During and after the la
officer in the Intelliger
intelligence duties. Since
advertising agency, a far
radio station and a PR cc
hurst, Kent, with his fami

Also by Ted Allbeury

Ted Allbeury

The Reaper

A MAYFLOWER BOOK

GRANADA
London Toronto Sydney New York

Published by Granada Publishing Limited in 1980

ISBN 0 583 13178 6

A Granada Paperback UK Original
Copyright © Ted Allbeury 1980

Granada Publishing Limited
Frogmore, St Albans, Herts AL2 2NF
and
3 Upper James Street, London W1R 4BP
866 United Nations Plaza, New York, NY 10017, USA
117 York Street, Sydney, NSW 2000, Australia
100 Skyway Avenue, Rexdale, Ontario, M9W 3A6, Canada
PO Box 84165, Greenside, 2034 Johannesburg, South Africa
61 Beach Road, Auckland, New Zealand

Set, printed and bound in Great Britain by
Cox & Wyman Limited, Reading
Set in Intertype Times

Granada ®
Granada Publishing ®

With love to Kay and Leslie Hersham
and David and Sarah.

Be not deceived; God is not mocked: for
whatsoever a man soweth, that shall he also reap.

Paul to the Galatians vi 7.

Chapter One

There are years when the news seems to consist of nothing but natural or man-made disasters. Wars, revolutions, earthquakes and floods kill hundreds of thousands, as if both man and nature had combined to alter the face of the earth. And there are years when the news is always of world importance but nobody gets hurt. 1953 was one of those years. Dwight D. Eisenhower was inaugurated as President of the USA, Stalin died, the USSR exploded its first hydrogen bomb, Everest was climbed, Queen Elizabeth II was crowned, and the UN signed an armistice with the North Koreans at Panmunjom.

On a more human level the English cricketers won the Ashes in Australia, and on 1 October, the Israelis celebrated Yom Kippur, and Frau Liselotte Woltmann gave birth to a daughter in a small town in Germany called Göttingen. It would have been nice to be able to say that they *celebrated* the birth of a daughter. But they were not that kind of people.

Göttingen had not been greatly damaged in the Allied air-raids, nor had there been a great deal of resistance before the surrender. The town still had most of its mediaeval buildings and its life revolved round its ancient university. Local people said that it was American and British respect for the university that had preserved the town itself. Herr Woltmann didn't give a damn why it was all, more or less, in one piece. By a miracle Kurt Woltmann had been put on a Wehrmacht hospital train when the Russian artillery was smashing the northern suburbs of Berlin. There had been the long and tortuous train journey to Hanover and in the grim military hospital they had taken off his shattered left leg just above the knee. His wife had been evacuated six months earlier to Hamburg. The Roman Catholic charity organization, Caritas, had eventually linked them together and the Hanover *Arbeitsamt* had found him a job as a metal-worker for one of the science faculties at the university in Göttingen.

The German economic miracle had got under way by 1953, and Kurt Woltmann had seen the extra responsibility of a child as the last straw for his overburdened back. He had suggested that the child should be put in an orphanage. But fate seemed against him even there. The orphanages were overflowing with real orphans, and none would accept a baby from a married couple where the man had a job.

As young Anna Woltmann grew up she was properly clothed and fed, but by the time she went to school she took it for granted that she was tolerated, not loved. She was a bright child and made friends at school, but on the few occasions when she brought friends home, her father's sharp tongue and her mother's silence ensured that the visits were never repeated. Anna Woltmann's parents became a joke. And as so often happens, gradually Anna Woltmann herself became a joke.

But somewhere in the genes of all those ancestors there was a stoic. By the time she was fifteen Anna Woltmann was a loner, she no longer looked for friendship outside her home or for affection inside it. When she was offered a place at the university she saw it as a reward for her independence. In fact, she had worked extremely hard. Unlike other girls there were no distractions to take her from her studies. Parents and backgrounds are of no significance to students so her parents were no longer a problem. She was pretty so she had invitations from young men. If they didn't interfere with her studies she accepted them, but the young men who dated her found her too independent. Nothing seemed to impress her. Expensive restaurants, concerts, wealthy backgrounds all were dismissed with that amused smile. She was always polite, but young men sensed that the politeness covered a sort of superiority. And for the life of them they couldn't see what she had to be superior about. She was pretty enough, that was why they dated her, but there were plenty of pretty girls in Germany. A surplus, in fact, of almost four or five to one. And her drab parents and background were a laughing stock. So why the superiority? It's not always easy when you are young, to distinguish between pride and an air of superiority. It's not all that easy when you are older.

It had been at the end of May when she was called to the Dean's office. It was the end of her second year and he had congratulated her on her work and said how sorry he was that she would not be taking the third year and her degree. It was an interview she was never going to forget.

'But I don't understand, Herr Professor. Why shouldn't I finish my degree course?'

He looked surprised. 'But surely your father discussed this with you.'

'Discussed what?'

'His letter.'

'I don't understand. Why should my father write to you?'

He slid the letter across his desk to her.

'You'd better read it, Fräulein Woltmann.'

She trembled as she sat reading the letter.

Sehr Geehrter Herr Professor Müller,

I have to inform you that my daughter Fräulein Anna Woltmann will not be able to continue her studies at the university in the Autumn. In the present economic circumstances of the Fatherland I find it impossible to continue to support her. We need her to be employed to make a contribution to the family exchequer.

    Yours

    K. Woltmann

She put it slowly back on his desk and stood up.

'Sit down for a moment, Fräulein Woltmann.'

9

He saw the white, stricken face, and for a moment he thought that she was going to faint.

'Perhaps the university could find sources of money for a loan to be repaid after you have graduated.'

'Thank you. But I wouldn't want that.'

'An Honours degree in French is a good qualification these days.'

She stood up and said quietly, 'Thank you for your help, Herr Professor.'

'If circumstances change . . .' he said.

'They won't.'

Outside, she sat on one of the benches under the lime trees. She had no doubts about the first thing she would do. And no idea what she would do after that.

She had walked back to the apartment and silently packed her few clothes and possessions in a cardboard case and a canvas hold-all. She hadn't spoken a word to her parents but had walked out of the house and down to the railway station. She had 45 marks in her handbag and she had left her belongings at the left-luggage office.

The 45 marks would get her to Stuttgart in the French Zone and then there would be enough for two weeks.

It was inconvenient that it was still light but she walked back into the town to the small street that housed the British Officers Club. Several of them looked at her amiably as she waited but it was almost ten o'clock before one of them spoke to her. He was a Canadian from Quebec and he had been amused that she spoke French. She had gone with him in his Jeep to his billet. A small house he shared with two other officers not far from the station. She had stayed with him that night, and as he lay between her legs she wondered if he realized that she had been a virgin. He was a friendly man and obviously found her attractive.

The next morning he had driven her to the station on his way to his office at Military Government HQ and the cigarettes in her canvas hold-all would keep her for ten days when they were sold on the black-market. She sold half of them before she paid for her ticket.

In Stuttgart she had found a small room and had only slept with one man before she found a job, translating documents for a French company starting up in Occupied Germany to manufacture domestic appliances. After a year she became personal assistant to the director and had moved to a small apartment near the centre of the town. Twice a year she had been able to make business trips to France. Sometimes to Strasbourg and once to Paris.

She had neither friends nor acquaintances, and sought none. And she made no attempts to contact her parents. Sometimes when she was tired from over-work she recalled that interview and still found it difficult to control her anger. Her heart would pound as she re-lived it. The callousness, the casualness with which her world had been smashed. The humiliation still stayed with her, mingled with a slow-burning hatred of her father.

Her employers were well satisfied to have such a single-minded and capable young woman on their staff and rewarded her accordingly. In 1978 part of her reward was a business trip to Paris that would leave her a week free for herself. She tried to keep the pleasure of thinking about the trip from her mind. It was part of the lesson she had learnt. Never rely on other people. Don't, even for a second, give them a chance to hurt you. She knew that she would find another betrayal, no matter how small, too much to bear.

On the first of her free days in Paris she had booked herself on to a guided tour round the buildings of the Sorbonne. The young man who had shown them round was a lecturer. Tall and slim with blond wavy hair, she thought his complexion dark enough to be a Corsican. And she was amused at his habit of almost continuously pushing his glasses back up his nose. She wondered why he didn't get the frames fixed. They were standing round him in the great lecture hall

11

when she noticed how quietly he spoke as he pointed out de Chavannes' painting. *The Sacred Wood*. And he was patient and forbearing with the foolish questions that some of them asked. He seemed to speak English, German and French equally fluently.

The tour took just over an hour and as he was handing them back to the driver he had asked if any of them taught languages or had language degrees. She cheated, for the first time in her life, and held up her hand. He smiled and said he would take her to the Collège de France, the 'three language college'.

He had stood with her, waving to the group on the bus as it drew away.

The Collège de France students learn to read the great Latin, Greek and Hebrew masterpieces and it was only when he translated one of the Hebrew texts on the wall that she realized he was a Jew. When he had suggested that they had a coffee together she had been delighted, and they had walked to a café in the rue Soufflot.

His subject was mediaeval French, and his research was on the documents of the European Guilds. She was much taken by his enthusiasm for his subjects and his eagerness to answer her questions. But even more she was impressed by the way he listened to what she had to say. He listened carefully, nodding sometimes, and when he thought she could be wrong he made his case as if she were an equal whose views were valuable. In the evening they had gone to see a re-run of *Un homme et une femme*.

It was as if some log-jam had been broken, some magic door opened. All that repressed but stored-up affection flowed out into the spring air. For the first time in her life she was happy, and for the first time in her life she felt safe with another human being. It would be untrue to say that she trusted him, the word never came to her mind.

The second day he had worked in the morning but in the afternoon they had picnicked in Fontainebleau. In the evening he had diffidently invited her to his small flat near the university. They had listened to music on his hi-fi and talked interminably but not about themselves. He made no sexual overtures but it was obvious that he found her desirable and when they walked down towards the river to find her a taxi his arm had gone round her waist as if it were a perfectly natural thing to do. Which it was.

She had lain in her bed that night thinking about him. His gentleness and his modesty, his ever-ready willingness to listen to her views and take them seriously. For almost any other pretty girl it would have been one of many such pleasant relationships, but for Anna Woltmann it was unique. And overwhelming. The emotions that a normal girl would have experienced over weeks or months, flooded out almost hour by hour and the warm-hearted young man responded willingly and affectionately. He was a loner too. But a different kind of loner. His independence came from a quiet self-confidence, from the background of a loving home and supportive parents, but he recognized this pretty girl's similar independance of spirit and her willingness to abandon her caution in her relationship with him. She lacked the brittleness of French girls of her age but he sensed the latent strength behind the pretty face and the melting brown eyes.

The day before she was due to return to Stuttgart they had walked in the sun in the Luxembourg Gardens. On a seat by the lake he had asked her to marry him. And when she said yes it was the first time that he had kissed her.

Up to that point, except for the speed, their courtship could have been out of some story by Daudet or Jane Austen. But that night they slept together and the following day they applied for a marriage licence, and she phoned through to her employers in Stuttgart who begged her to come back for a few weeks. She thought they were mad. That existence had gone for ever. She moved her things from the hotel to his rooms, and they talked all day. They even faced a few facts. Like the problems of a Jew marrying a German. And jobs. And money. But lovers can be merciless with facts.

13

He had phoned his father to tell him the news and they met him that evening at his apartment in the rue la Fayette.

His father was a sophisticated man more avuncular than fatherly, and she found it impossible to tell whether he approved or not of his son's sudden decision. He was charming with her, but she guessed that he was charming with all women, and most men. He asked no questions. They were adults with their own lives to lead, their own decisions to make. There were things to be sorted out later, but weddings come first.

She knew after that meeting that she was going to be cherished. She was going to live happily ever after.

Anna Woltmann and Paul Simon were married in a civil ceremony on the first Saturday in June, on a sunny day, in Paris.

Chapter Two

The plane's wing dipped as they went low over the frontier and turned to follow the river. Sitting alongside the pilot he could see the white sand where the torrent had trimmed small spits of land off the banks so that the forest rose up sheer from the water's edge. Even from a hundred feet the tops of the trees looked like a lush green fleece laid over the land as far as the eye could see. No tracks relieved the solid green. But twenty minutes later he saw the sandy clearing as they circled, the three huts and the short landing-strip.

They sat in the plane until the clouds of dust settled, and when the pilot pushed back the canopy he could smell the dank heat of the forest like an overheated greenhouse. The fuselage was shimmering in the heat and he licked his hands before he grabbed the handle to jump down to the ground.

He stood for a few moments, looking around, stretching his jaw to clear his ears. What a godforsaken place it was. What a life for a man. And now they had to fight back even to stay in a hell-hole like this. His life at the sun-baked monastery was bad enough, but this was what the very outskirts of hell must be like.

He saw Altman walking towards him. An old jacket slung loosely round his shoulders, his khaki slacks stained and crumpled, tucked into worn leather riding boots. A far cry now from the bustling Standartenführer who had lorded it over the population of occupied Lyon. Every time he saw him Altman behaved as if the war had never ended in defeat. There had been a time when he even wore his medals at their meetings. Not just the ribbons, but the decorations themselves, awkwardly pinned on to a shirt or a jacket. And he had not been amused when they joked about it. Then he could see that one of Altman's eyes was closed, the lower lid

15

puffed and livid. He was holding his head slightly to one side so that he could look ahead with his good eye. As Altman stumbled forward he was holding out his hand to his visitor.

Kleiber took the proffered hand. 'What the hell's the matter with your eye, Fritz?'

'A wasp sting. It's nothing. Listen, that must be Heinz.'

As they stood listening they heard the clatter of the helicopter from the south-west. It circled twice before it landed at the far end of the rough air-strip. The pilot slid out first and reached up to help his passenger jump to the ground. He was a tall lean man, deeply tanned with grey hair cut close to his scalp. When he turned and saw them he waved his arm and picked up his canvas hold-all.

As they walked to the smaller hut two Indian men stood to attention as the white men passed them. Altman gave them a half-hearted salute and they stood at ease as the Germans went up the short flight of wooden steps to the hut.

Inside, the light was dim except where termite holes let in bright rays of sunshine. There was a table and four chairs, a sideboard whose doors hung part open. An old iron bed was pushed into the corner under a mosquito net that had been repaired again and again with rough untidy stitches. There was a smell of oil and putrid food.

Altman stood awkwardly, trying to see the other two out of his one good eye.

'Are either of you staying the night?'

'No. I've got to be back before dark, Fritz.'

Altman shrugged. 'What about you, Otto?'

Kleiber hesitated and then said reluctantly, 'I'll stay till tomorrow, Fritz. Give you company for one night.'

They sat talking for almost an hour and then Altman stood up, walked to the door and shouted something. When he sat back at the table, Kleiber said, 'Were you talking Quechua?'

'Yes. The stupid bastards can't even speak rough Spanish.'

'How did you pick it up?'

Altman grinned. 'A sleeping dictionary, my friend. You'll see her when she brings the beer.' He turned his face awkwardly towards Kleiber. 'I can fix one for you tonight, Otto.'

A young girl came in carrying a tray and four tumblers set in a bowl of water. She was a pale brown, with thick, black hair bobbed at her shoulders, and a fringe. She wasn't pretty but her features were neat. Apart from a narrow ribbon across her belly and five long-beaded necklaces which hung between her small breasts she was naked. Her body was smooth and lithe, and her legs strong and sturdy.

Solemn-faced she took out the tumblers from the cold water and put them on the table. Altman spoke to her, smiling, and the girl nodded without looking up.

Altman turned to Kleiber. 'I told her she'll be looking after you tonight, Otto.'

'How old is she, Fritz?'

'God knows. Old enough to give you what you want anyway.'

'Ask her how old she is.'

Altman spoke to the girl and she shrugged as she answered him.

'She's not sure. She thinks she's thirteen,'

Heinz Rauch said sharply, 'Let's get on with it, Fritz.'

Altman resented the unspoken reprimand, the attempt to give him orders, and he grinned at Kleiber. 'I think our Heinz prefers what he gets at the convent, eh?'

But he nodded a dismissal to the girl and looked across at the others.

'If we don't do something they'll never give us any peace.'

Heinz Rauch said, 'They'll never give us any peace whatever we do; but the significant factor is the age group they're using now.'

Altman frowned. 'What's that got to do with it, Heinz?'

Rauch stifled his impatience and said slowly, 'Until two years ago the Jews who were after us were our own age. People who were involved with the old days. Now they are using their children. There was a time when we could feel

17

that as we all grew older we were safer. That's gone. And for members still in Europe it means that their children could be targets now. If *we* don't do something, then they will. I want control to stay with us.'

Kleiber put down his glass. 'Shall we get the funds, Heinz?'

Altman smashed his hand down on the table in a show of anger. 'If the Monsignor doesn't agree I'll raise the funds in Germany.'

Rauch looked coldly at Altman. 'Your name wouldn't raise a thousand marks, my friend. Keep your play-acting for the Indians or we're going to quarrel.' Rauch turned to Kleiber. 'He will fund us. He has already raised the money in Europe. It won't take all that much.'

'Do you think it will stop the Jews?'

Rauch sighed. 'God knows. I shouldn't think so. But if we just sit here then they'll finish us off one by one. We've got to start hitting back. Show them that it will cost them lives too. Why should we just sit around to be killed or kidnapped every time they want some publicity?'

Altman pushed back his chair and walked to the cupboard. He came back with a notepad and flung it on the table. Sitting down heavily he said, 'I've done a list. All good men.' He pushed the notepad over to Rauch who read it in silence. When he looked up he looked at Altman.

'I don't know Trommer. Who is he? What did he do?'

'Hauptsturmführer at Race and Resettlement HQ. He farms now in Portugal. Oranges, lemons and vineyards. He's helped us with money, and he's sheltered people for us on half a dozen occasions. He's totally accepted in Portugal.'

Rauch shoved the pad across to Kleiber who read the list of names.

'Six is too many, Fritz. I'd say four at the outside.'

Altman shrugged. 'OK. Let it be four. When do you want it to start?'

It was Rauch who spoke. 'How soon can you start?'

Altman leaned back in his chair. 'Tomorrow.'

'OK. Start right away.'

Altman clapped his hands together, grinning.

'Jesus. It's like the old days. We'll teach those bastards another lesson.' He stood up. 'I'll tell the girls to fix a bed for you, Otto.'

When they were alone Kleiber said, 'Don't grind him down, Heinz. I know he's a pain in the arse, but his name counts in Europe.'

Rauch shrugged. 'He's not just a pain in the arse, Otto. He's an oaf, an antique action-man. I remember looking at his personal file in Berlin when we had had complaints from Vichy. He was screwing schoolgirls then, and now . . .' He waved his arm round the room '. . . he sits here day after day like a rat in a trap, pretending that he is controlling the fate of ODESSA. He daren't leave here because he knows the Jews would get him. He's a prime target. Just keep him under control, that's all we ask. Some of us have to live in the real world.' He smiled. 'And apart from that we're getting old.'

Altman and Kleiber walked with Rauch to the helicopter and waited until it circled and headed south over the forest.

As they walked back it was cooler, and the sun was setting behind the *hevea* trees. The air was full of flying insects so that they constantly fanned their hands to keep off the poisonous predators, the pium who bred in the river giving way to the large sand-flies and midges that came from the stands of thick bamboo and Buriti palms.

Altman said, 'A real shit, our Heinz,' and he looked at Kleiber with his one good eye for agreement. 'Still thinks he's sitting in Albrechtstrasse fighting the Reds and the Abwehr.'

'I wouldn't underrate him, Fritz, if I were you. And I shouldn't make cracks about the Monsignore, either. Somebody could pass the word back to him.'

Altman snorted. 'I couldn't give a stuff about Bormann, he's as vulnerable as the rest of us.'

19

'He funds you, my friend. He expects loyalty for that.'

'And he gets it too. When they want action it's me they turn to.'

'OK. Just remember what I've said, that's all.'

Altman grinned at him. 'I've told the girl to fix you up in the small hut. There's no light unfortunately, but you won't need one. I've taught that little bitch every trick in the book. She'll let you do anything you want.'

Kleiber smiled and put his arm round Altman's shoulder. 'You're a lucky bastard, Fritz. You've got it made down here. You were always the same.'

Altman laughed. 'Ten hours a day I worked, rounding those yids up and loading them on the trains. I'd pick out a couple of young bitches and have 'em that night. They thought it would save their kids or their daddies, letting me put it up 'em. Fought like bloody tigers some of them. I screwed more than two hundred in nine months. Those were the days.' He stood still looking at Kleiber. 'You know I still can't believe we lost. How in hell did it all fall apart, Otto?'

'Forget it, Fritz. It's more than thirty years ago.'

Altman sighed deeply. 'I'll never forget it, Otto. We were the masters. How did we let it all go?'

The young girl had slid into the ramshackle bed with Kleiber and in the darkness he had fondled the smooth, firm, young body. When he was sufficiently aroused he pulled her to him. And through the night he had her again and again when the jungle silence and the heat had woken him.

After the last time the girl slept beside him as he lay open-eyed in the darkness thinking. Altman was an oaf but he said out loud the things they all thought to themselves. How *had* it all fallen apart. Everything Hitler had said had been proved right. Even now when the West had seen what the Reds were after they gave no acknowledgment to the Führer. And now the Jews had Israel; and German chancellors sat at conference tables with them. And the German people worked to pay reparations to the Jews who had been

their downfall. Men like Bormann had their Vatican pass-
ports, living in jungle monasteries, frightened that the Jew
hunters would find them. Age brought them no peace. The
ODESSA would have to bring back the balance. They had
to strike back or the Jews and Zionists would winkle them
out one by one. Not just in South America, but in all the
countries of Europe. Men who had put the past behind
them, who were now accepted and prospering in their com-
munities, would be hounded into the courts for the sake of
Jewish propaganda. Altman was the man to do it. He would
motivate the comrades who were still in Europe. It was for
all their sakes. The world would learn that you didn't attack
the ODESSA and get away with it. That was how the Israelis
played it. And two could play at that game.

Chapter Three

It depends on how old you are as to how you judge the Place de la Contrescarpe. It wasn't all that long ago when it was reckoned to be one of the toughest corners of the Left Bank. Hard, violent and villainous. Even these days you can still see tramps sleeping on the pavement. But as often happens in Paris the character of a back-street or square can be changed overnight by some innovation, and when the restaurant called the *'Requin Chagrin'* modernized itself and specialized in the cuisine of Réunion, the *Place* itself took on a new life. In the daytime it maintained its old-fashioned image but at night its ambience changed. Prices went up to keep the students out and it found its clientele from the 16th arrondissement.

On the far side of the Square was a house that had survived without its ground-floor being turned into a shop. It was only a matter of time; but now it housed a young couple, a writer and his mistress, and an elderly couple and their two grandchildren.

The young couple were Paul and Anna Simon. Two years married now. He was still a lecturer at the Sorbonne and she had given up her own job as an interpreter a month earlier. She was secure enough now in her marriage to be mildly critical from time to time of the young man's lack of ambition. He generally smiled as he listened and then asked her what form his ambition should take. Should it be for more money, a professorship, or perhaps Greek as an additional language. He never really argued, but somehow he always seemed to win the mild verbal tussles. Perhaps he would change when the baby came.

They had a small circle of friends, mainly colleagues of his from the Sorbonne or the Collège de France. Young men and women who were faintly but nicely amused at the domesticity of the young couple. They had nicknamed her 'la Tigresse' because she would defend her husband with open hostility at even the mildest disagreement with his views. There were many who envied them their obvious compatibility and their self-assurance that it would always be the same. The more perceptive ones recognized that the girl's self-assurance was based entirely on her husband's love and affection.

In four months' time the child would be born. Pierre, after his grandfather, if it was a boy. Adrienne, after nobody in particular, if it was a girl. And today was his birthday. The 15th, the Ides of March. And he was 30.

She took one last look round the room. She had a slight feeling of guilt that she had not invited any of their friends, but she wanted him to herself. The table was laid, the two red candles pristine and waiting to be lit. There was a damp cloth over the bowl of fresh strawberries. A wild extravagance but they were his favourite fruit. The fresh salmon was in its bowl of lettuce in the kitchen and the cold consommé en gelée was in the refrigerator. The cassette with the Max Bruch violin concerto on one side and the Mendelssohn on the other side was in its pink paper. The leather-bound Larousse was still in the shop's packing because it was so neat. And the small cube was on his plate. The signet ring in gold, with his initials intertwined with hers and inside the inscription – 'Je t'aime jusq'au bout de ma vie'.

She walked to the window and looked out. She saw him immediately, his fair hair lifting in the wind, his red tie flying over his shoulder, his jacket open. The idiot would catch his death of cold. He was carrying something in his hand, a square parcel tied with red ribbon in a fancy bow. Then he was under the window and she heard the street-bell ring.

She opened the door and stood on the landing, leaning over the banister. He had stopped to talk to the concierge. She was wishing him a happy birthday and he laughed as he asked her how she knew. There were cards for him, she said,

23

and two parcels. Then he was walking up the stairs towards her. He must have sensed that she was there because he looked up, smiling.

She heard no noise, she saw no flash, as the front of the house blew out. The masonry seemed to hang in mid-air for several moments until it fell like a curtain, a waterfall of stone, bricks, glass and furniture.

When the inquest was held she had not been there. She was still in a coma at the hospital. The inquest had been on Paul Simon, the concierge, and a young man who had been killed in the street by the falling masonry. A verdict was brought in of 'death caused by explosives concealed in a parcel and sent by a person or persons unknown'. The police were diligently pursuing their inquiries.

Chapter Four

The young *infirmière* and the *surveillante* stood looking at the girl in the bed. Her black hair was lank and dull and a nerve quivered continuously at the corner of one eye. One arm was bandaged to a rail and a drip ran down to her arm. A white plastic tube led between her lips, and a clear tube came from one nostril.

The young girl whispered. 'Do you think she knows, sister?'

'Of course not, girl. How can she know, she's not been conscious since she came in.'

'Do you think she'll die?'

'The old man in the men's ward will die if you don't take him his *bassin*.'

The young girl still lingered. 'Who will tell her if she recovers?'

'The almoner. Now get on your way.'

It was almost a month later when they told her that she had lost her child and that her husband was dead. It was the physician who told her and he held her hand as he broke the news. She had swallowed once, otherwise there had been no reaction. No tears, no words.

Even two weeks later when she was physically almost normal she still did not speak. When she was forced to answer she nodded or shook her head, and her eyes seemed to be focused on something far away.

The first and only visitor who was allowed to see her was her father-in-law.

Pierre Simon was a large man, bearded, moving more easily than his bulk suggested. He had inherited the family textile business and had immediately sold it for a large sum.

He had opened a small gallery in Paris and from the profits of that enterprise he had bought a hotel in Nice. His friends said that he had a magic touch, his rivals constantly looked for a skeleton in the cupboard. His charm and intellect had won him many friends and they had stayed with him until 1940. Then his wife was taken by the Germans to Ravensbrück. He was taken to Belsen-Bergen. When the concentration camp was over-run by the British Army in 1945 Pierre Simon weighed nine stone. But if you survived at all, that was enough. After two months in hospital he had gone looking for his wife. When the authorities could do nothing he had started to search himself. Except for troops and administrators, no foreigners, no matter how important, were allowed into Occupied Germany, but if you had money enough, and motive enough, there were ways and means. Pierre Simon had both. He had bribed an American at the Document Centre to let him examine the Gestapo records that registered the dispatch of prisoners to the camps. He had found, and kept, the original document that had consigned his wife and 224 other women to Ravensbrück. A year later he had paid a Russian Army doctor in gold to arrange the release of his wife from a displaced persons camp near Magdeburg.

For three years he had stayed with her at the villa just outside Aix. Walking with her, talking continuously to bring her back into the world. They never spoke of what had happened to either of them. Neither of them could have borne the other's pain. She had been sitting with him in the sunshine on the patio when she first smiled. He was reading her Daudet's 'Lettres de mon moulin' when it happened, and he had slowly closed the book and put it to one side. A year later she had given birth to their son. He was an unspoken symbol of their new life and they loved him openly but with good sense. He was not to be a sacrificial lamb to their nightmare years.

His business life he took in his stride; being decisive and shrewd, most of his ventures prospered. When they didn't there were few regrets and no mourning. You may learn more about business at Harvard or the Polytèchnique but you learn about priorities and life in Belsen.

His wife had died when their son was 24, peacefully, and, thanks to the drugs, painlessly. The lesions on her kidneys and spleen had no doubt played their part. He had been lonely but he had kept his sorrow to himself. He sold all the enterprises that required his personal touch and kept on his apartment in the rue la Fayette. From time to time he travelled, sometimes to London, frequently to Vienna.

When his son had announced that he was to marry a German girl the shock had been almost physical, and it had taken all his strength and resources to hide his distress. It had seemed at first a kind of disloyalty to marry a double enemy. An enemy of the French and an enemy of the Jews. But when he saw them together the resentment had gone. She hadn't even been born when the Nazis were around and she seemed to give the young man a cutting edge that he had lacked before. She would make a good matriarch and there would be spirit in her children.

When the police notified him of his son's death he had no doubt as to why he had died.

When he was shown into the white room at the hospital the girl was asleep. He pulled up a chair beside her bed and waited.

It was an hour before her eyes opened, looking up at the ceiling to where a lampshade moved slowly in a breeze from the open window.

Five minutes later she turned her head slowly to look at him.

'Don't talk, Anna. I'll come to see you again tomorrow. Maybe we can talk then.'

She nodded.

'I've talked to the doctor,' he said. 'He feels that perhaps in one week you could be discharged. When that time comes I shall bring the car and we'll go down to Aix. The country food and the country air will be good for you. I would like

27

your company. Perhaps you could spare me a few weeks of your time. I've brought you something to read, *ma chère.*'

He laid a book beside her hand on the bed. It was Montaigne's Essays. There was a slip of paper marking Book Two and the essay on 'The affection of fathers for their children'.

He waited until the next evening before he went back to see her. She was sitting up in bed and the book lay open beside her.

As he pulled up the chair alongside the bed she said, '*Beau-père?*'

'Yes, my love. What is it?'

'It won't make me happy if I go to the villa at Aix.'

'Of course not. Nothing will make us happy for a long, long time. All we do at Aix is to get well enough to be unhappy. To sigh in the fresh air is better than to sigh here.' And he waved his hand at the room.

She looked at his face and her lips trembled.

'Tell me it didn't happen, *beau-père.*'

He reached out his hand for hers.

'It happened my love. I've rung your number a dozen times in the hope that it was just a dream.' He turned her hand so that its palm locked with his. 'Did Paul tell you of his mother and me in wartime?'

She shook her head. 'No, we never talked about the war. We never thought about it.'

He nodded. 'Of course. Even for me it seems a long time ago. Or maybe it never happened. There are always proverbs to cover our lives. Unfortunately they are banal. But fortunately they are often true. Only time will heal this wound. You won't believe that right now. Take comfort that I once didn't believe it, maybe twice. It was true nevertheless.' He started to sigh and then caught his breath. 'When shall we go, *ma chère?*'

She turned to look at his face. 'Is tomorrow too soon?'

He stood up. 'I'll be here at noon.'

There had been very little left at the bombed house. The firemen had made a small pile of broken and burnt furniture and household goods from the Simon apartment and covered it with a canvas sheet. There was a cardboard box with the charred remnants of photographs and papers. Pierre Simon looked through them and then gave orders for them all to be taken away to the salvage depôt. He knew from experience that the less that remained the better.

He had checked with the ward-sister the sizes of the clothes the girl would need, and had bought her new things himself, choosing them carefully so that they were neither dowdy nor exciting.

When at last the loose white woollen coat was wrapped round her she took his arm and walked slowly down the hospital steps to the waiting car.

He had hired a plane to fly them to Aix and sent his chauffeur and car on ahead.

It was 5 o'clock in the evening when they bounced down into the meadow of one of the neighbouring farms. His own estate manager was waiting for them with a pony and an old-fashioned cabriolet, varnished and painted in its original colours. As they trotted briskly through the country lanes he pointed out the minor landmarks and pretended not to notice her sighs. He said nothing that could remind her of his son, and talked only of the present.

He felt her trembling as they walked up the stone steps to the villa. The hospital had given him sleeping tablets for her, and after she had taken two he left her with the housekeeper to undress. When she was in bed he went back into the room, standing at the bay-window talking. Talking of nothing but giving her no time to think. She was asleep in ten minutes and he walked back slowly down the stairs. He had done this all before, but it wasn't any easier the second time.

By the middle of the second week she was walking round the estate by herself, but always he was waiting for her to return, to check how she looked. There was going to be a day when she would want to talk.

It was four weeks before that happened. They were having dinner together, a cool breeze blowing the curtains at the doors to the patio, the perfume of mimosa in the room. When he had poured them a final glass of wine she said quietly, 'Tell me about what happened?'

He stood up. 'Let's sit in the sunshine and I'll tell you.'

He pulled up the wicker chairs so that they sat side by side, his chair slightly turned so that he could just see her face without turning his head.

'There was a bomb in the parcel that the concièrge gave him. It had been handed in to her an hour before Paul got home. It exploded as he walked up the stairs. The house was a ruin. There was nothing left. By a miracle only two other people were killed.'

'They mistook Paul for somebody else?'

'No. I'm afraid not. It was meant to kill him.'

Softly, barely audibly, she said, 'Why?'

'For two reasons. Firstly, he was a Jew.'

There was a long silence and then she said, 'And secondly?'

'Have you ever heard of an organization called the Jewish International Documentation Centre?'

'No.'

'Do you remember when Eichmann was kidnapped and brought to Israel to stand trial?'

'Vaguely.'

'The Centre in Vienna traces Nazis who were responsible for murdering and torturing Jews. Others take action on this information.'

'But what's that got to do with Paul?'

'You remember that sometimes Paul went away for a day or two?'

'But that was for research. He told me that.'

'It was research for the organization in Vienna. He was particularly competent at tracing documents that would provide evidence. He did a lot of things. I won't go into the details.'

'So who killed him?'

Pierre Simon closed his eyes. 'An organization called ODESSA. Have you ever heard of it?'

'No.'

'They are a group of top Nazis. Most of them are in South America. They funded and protected the war criminals who escaped or went underground after the war.'

'But what's that got to do with Paul? He wasn't even born then.'

'The Documentation Centre in Vienna tracks them down. Paul was helping them. He was one of their most efficient operators.'

'Why didn't he tell me about this?'

'I expect he didn't want you to be involved. There were other reasons too.'

'Like what?'

'Because they were Germans he was tracing. He thought you might be upset about that.'

'Did he talk with you about all this?'

'Only once. I told him that I agreed that you should not be told.'

'And these people paid someone to kill Paul? Just like that?'

'They didn't need to pay anyone. They could do it themselves. If you were SS or Gestapo or Sicherheitsdienst you don't need others to do your killing for you.'

'How do you know that this is what happened?'

'The people in Vienna told me. They had killed somebody else before they killed Paul.'

'Do you know who actually planted the bomb?'

'They know it was organized by one of four men. They don't know which one. They'll find out in due course.'

She turned in her chair to look at him. 'You mean to say that somebody just decided to kill Paul because he worked for this organization in Vienna?'

'They are frightened people now, Anna. They're old, getting older. They're beginning to panic.'

'For Christ's sake, *beau-père*, he was your son. How can you sit there and talk so calmly?'

'Would it make any difference if I shouted, my dear?'

She sank back into the chair. 'Christ. The bastards.'

'There was something I wanted to mention to you, Anna.'

She sighed. 'What was that?'

'I've opened a bank account for you. You won't have to worry about money, ever.'

She turned to look at him and she stretched out her hand to touch his arm. 'You're such a good man, Pierre.'

'You won't have to worry about that sort of thing – ever.'

'Do you know who these four men are?'

'Yes.'

'Tell me.'

'It wouldn't do any good, my dear.'

She sat in silence in the evening sunshine looking down the slope of the hill, past the vineyards to the lake. There was a rowing boat tied up to the small island in the centre of the lake and a boy sat on the bank with his arms round a girl as he kissed her.

She shivered and stood up, wrapping the woollen shawl round her shoulders.

'Will you tell me about Paul – I mean when he was a small boy in this house?'

He stood up clumsily, looking at her face. 'Are you sure, Anna? Won't it upset you?'

'I'm sure it will, but I'd rather think about him here than keep seeing him walk across the *Place* in Paris.'

She covered her face with her hands, shaking her head, and Pierre Simon stood there awkwardly. When she put down her hands he saw the tears on her cheeks as she looked up at him.

'Would you like to sleep in the room Paul had when he was here?'

She nodded.

When the housekeeper had left, the girl looked round the

32

room. It was a very simple room, white walls and a pale brown fitted carpet. The divan bed had two white pillows and a duvet with a faded pattern of field poppies and cornflowers. The small cottage-type window looked out on to the back of the house, across the netted fruit garden to the two greenhouses and the brick wall that enclosed the garden from the hillside. She could just see the waterfall where it sparkled and splashed at the rocky outcrop on the edge of the wood.

There was a small open bookcase. Text books, boys' adventure stories, two or three books of poetry, one of Verlaine. Then the war-horses of Zola, Rousseau, Baudelaire, a paperback of Jean-Paul's *Le Défi Américain*, and a hardback of the *Family of Man*. A few foreign language dictionaries, a Hebrew grammar, a cluster of travel books and, surprisingly, a tattered copy of *Aimez-vous Brahms*?

On a shelf was a painted plastic model of a Spitfire on a stand, and a Mirage half finished and unpainted. There were some sea-shells, a few smooth stones and a piece of polished pyrites. Above the shelf were half a dozen photographs pinned to a cork board. There was one of Paul aged about 10, sitting solemn-faced on a pony. A portrait of a pretty woman with eyes that were either alert or fearful, she couldn't tell which. A group of children standing around a maypole, each holding a ribbon, Paul at the far side of the circle, head on one side, smiling. These photographs were arranged around one central photograph. It showed a line of women and children in torn, bedraggled clothes, standing in line facing the camera. A small boy with a gaunt skeleton of a face stood with one foot on the other, staring at the camera with big solemn eyes, his hand reaching up to hold his mother's skirt. There were no tears on any of the faces, just utter despair. The despair that comes when all hope has gone that miracles will happen or prayers be answered. Although the SS officer had his back to the camera you could just see the 'Death's Head' skull of the 'Totenkopf' Division on his collar patch.

As she realized that it was a photograph of Jews being lined up for the gas chambers she saw the strip of paper and the caption in Paul's writing that said *'N'oubliez jamais'*.

Her fists clenched in anger as she stared at the photograph. The men who had decided in cold-blood to have her husband murdered were the same as the men in the photograph who looked with indifference on the sad, helpless women and children who were only minutes away from extinction. No wonder Paul had helped to track them down. That scrawled message under the photograph said so much about the gentle young man. And she saw him again, walking across the *Place*, blond hair and red tie blowing in the wind. Dear, gentle Paul who had a pain in his heart that she had never known about. Who said nothing, because she was a German; and he loved her.

Then she felt the effect of the sleeping pills and there was no time even to undress. She lay on the bed and pulled the pillows to her face as the room swung slowly in the first waves of sleep. She dreamt that she was on a train from Göttingen to Stuttgart.

Chapter Five

Pierre Simon noticed that she was not wearing a dress when she came down mid-morning. She was wearing a loose sweater and the jeans he had bought for her. Then he realized that the sweater was an old one of Paul's that she must have taken from his wardrobe. He made no comment as he sat reading his post at the far end of the table while she ate her breakfast.

'Will you tell me what happened to you and your wife during the war, *beau-père*?'

He looked up, surprised, and caught unprepared. He sat silently for long moments, looking at her face. He sighed, then shook his head slowly. 'I couldn't. I couldn't bear to think of it. And I couldn't say it. Not even for you, my dear.'

'You told Paul?'

'Yes. It seemed to be a duty. I didn't tell him all.'

'Was he upset?'

'Yes. For a week or more he didn't speak at all. He went for walks on his own. There was no comfort I could give him.'

'And after the week?'

'Something changed in him. I think that that was when he first started working for the Documentation Centre.'

'Do you wish now that you hadn't told him?'

He looked away from her to the sunshine and bougain-villaea that flooded the patio. When he looked back at her he said gently, 'As a father it breaks my heart, but no, I don't regret telling him. What happened to my wife and me happened to millions of Jews. Our children have a right to know.'

'Doesn't that breed hate?'

He looked at her. 'Yes. But it is right to hate those people.'

'Germans?'

He sighed. 'That's the temptation of course, but no, not Germans, just Nazis.'

'Why not all Germans?'

He half-smiled. 'Maybe three reasons. Mendelssohn was a German as well as a Jew. Secondly, there were thousands of Germans in the concentration camps, they were exterminated too. And thirdly there are those Germans like you, who weren't even born when all that was going on.' He looked down at the table then back at her face. 'You loved my Paul and that's all that matters.'

'Who were the four men, Pierre?'

'Why do you want to know?'

'I just want to know.'

He shook his head. 'No. There's no point in knowing, Anna. It makes it worse to know that they are alive. They are animals, savages. They always were, they always will be. Their fate will overtake them one day.'

'Will the people in Vienna do anything about them?'

He gathered up his mail and stood up. 'They are men who are protected, Anna. The Centre brings men to court, to justice. We have never been executioners. Their names will go down on the lists. If evidence is ever uncovered then they can be tried.'

'Do you think evidence *will* be found?'

He shook his head. 'It's not likely, Anna. The Centre hasn't got those kind of resources.' He half turned. 'What are you going to do today?'

'Just walk.'

He nodded and bent across the table to kiss her head.

She walked down to the valley and up into the woods to sit on the rocks by the waterfall. She sat there with her elbows on her knees, her chin resting on her hands, her eyes closed as she thought. It reminded her of when she had sat on the bench outside the university, only half-believing that her life could have been smashed up so callously and casually. Just a

36

brief letter ended her studies. No reference to her, just a few scribbled lines. But she had known then what she had to do. She had dreaded the consequences, the insecurity, the isolation, the complete lack of background support. She had sworn she would never leave herself open again for others to decide her fate. But meeting Paul had changed all that. It had seemed that it would go on for ever. Never for a moment had she thought it would end. She dreamt so many times in that lonely room in Stuttgart of revenging herself on her father. For months she had wished him dead.

But all that was nothing compared with this. To plan cold-bloodedly to kill a man. Indifferent to his death and the death of others. Because he was a Jew and because he traced documents that might incriminate murderers. This was what people meant when they talked about Nazis. If this is what they did when they were defeated, God knows what they must have been like when they were in total power. She had sometimes wondered why the Jews hadn't fought back but she knew now. She knew how she felt when she had been betrayed by her parents. Despite what they said, the world had betrayed the Jews. They made a few gestures but they left them to their fate. She knew how they must have felt. But what a difference it would have made if every Jew who died had taken a Nazi with him. She remembered the photograph on Paul's bedroom wall, and she wanted to scream. They should have killed back. Like it said in the Bible – an eye for an eye, a tooth for a tooth. All it needed was anger. And in that moment it was as if all the world was silent as her eyes closed and her fists clenched. When she opened her eyes the world came back again, the wood-pigeons were still cooing and she could hear the lambs at the far end of the valley. But it was a different world, because she knew what she was going to do. She had no idea how she was going to do it, no more than she knew what she was going to do when she walked out of her father's house. They would say it was ridiculous because she was a woman, a housewife. But what better cover could she have than that. She would do it. Not

37

just for herself and Paul, but for all the Jews like those in the photograph. The ones who couldn't strike back. She could, by God, and she would.

There was a touchstone. An omen that could decide the issue for her. She would put it to the test. She stood up and brushed the earth from the seat of her jeans.

She called out as she entered the house but there was no reply. She called again and waited. But there was still no answer. His small office was on the far side of the hall and she walked across and tried the door. It opened and she walked inside. There was nobody there.

There was a modern teak desk and three steel filing cabinets. On the desk was that day's mail. She looked through it quickly. Share certificates, two company reports, an involved letter from the tax office at Marseilles, an invitation to a *vernissage* at a gallery in Fréjus, and a letter in Italian that she couldn't read.

She turned to the filing cabinets. The keys were in the locks, the duplicates hanging loosely on their rings. It was in the furthest one that she found the file marked 'Dok. Zentrum Wien'. She slid out the file and opened it flat. It was the third letter and she felt faint as she read it. It referred to a telephone conversation and it gave the names and locations of the four men. It was written in German. She took the file to the desk and reached for the pad by the telephone.

She wrote in capitals the details she wanted.

1 STEIN, HANS. AMSTERDAM, NEDERLANDS. KUNSTHANDLER. EHEMALIGER ANGEHORIGER GEHEIMESTAATSPOLIZEI. FRANKREICH UND POLEN.

2 TROMMER, WILHELM. ALBUFEIRA, PORTUGAL. GROSSGUTBESITZER. EHEMALIGER MAJOR DER GEHEIMFELDPOLIZEI. NEDERLANDS UND POLEN.

3 MULLER WALTHER. SOUTH CROYDON, ENG-

LAND. PHOTOHANDLUNG EHEMALIGER SS-OBERSTURMBANNFUHRER REICHSSICH-ERHEITSHAUPTAMT BERLIN, UND OST-FRONT.
4 JANSEN, LUDWIG. AURORA, CHICAGO, USA. BAUUNTERNEHMER EHEMALIGER SS-STURMBANNFUHRER TOTENKOPF VER-BAND. KZ BELSEN-BERGEN, POLEN UND REGIMENT BRANDENBERG.

She slid the file back in the cabinet, her heart beating and her hands trembling. Walking to the door seemed to take a tremendous effort. As she closed the door behind her she heard noises from the patio and she walked quietly upstairs to her room, the folded paper in her hand.

As she sat on the bed she was panting. If this was how she felt after doing that simple act how could she possibly carry on with her plan? Involuntarily she shook her head to push away her doubts.

She had a drink with Pierre on the patio and when they got up to go into dinner she said casually, 'Could I borrow the car tomorrow to go into Aix?'

'Of course. And while you are there go into the Banque de France and ask for the manager. He'll give you a pass-book for your account.'

She parked near the Place de Verdun and walked to the bank. The manager told her that there was 50,000 francs on deposit for her which would be topped up monthly. And in addition, there was an order to pay into her current account 1800 francs a week.

She walked to the public library and sat in the reference section leafing through old newspaper files. She also listed the titles of books on the Resistance and the Maquis.

There was a name that kept cropping up in the Marseilles area. The man was an Englishman but his name was French.

Duchamps. Alexander Duchamps, and the records said that he had settled in Le Cannet after the war as the owner of a small hotel.

She checked in the telephone directory at the Post Office. It said Duchamps A. Hotel de Lorraine, Le Cannet 45963.

At the café she called the number. The receptionist said she would find *le patron.*

'Duchamps. Qui parle?'

'My name is Anna Simon, M. Duchamps. I wanted to ask if you have a single room for tomorrow night.'

'I'm afraid not. There's a double if you would care to take that.'

She hesitated for only a moment. 'Yes please, just for one night.'

'Fine. What time will you be arriving?'

'About mid-day.'

'Good. It'll be ready for you by then.'

She hung up the phone slowly and bowed her head to touch the coldness of the glass window, and she thought for a moment that she might be going mad.

That night she sat on her bed looking at the concentration camp photograph. She had asked Pierre for the car and when he had agreed she told him she was staying the next night at Le Cannet. He had seemed pleased that she was capable of being on her own for a day and a night.

Chapter Six

The Hotel de Lorraine was a rambling collection of buildings that had been added to the original hotel as the business prospered. A young man came out to help her with her bag and show her where to park the car.

M. Duchamps himself registered her arrival, and a few minutes later she was shown to her room and a maid brought in a tray of biscuits and coffee. The room itself was not a traditional hotel room, more like a room in a house. Net curtains waved idly at the open windows, there was a table and three armchairs, and a radio on a small table at the side of the bed.

About twenty minutes later Duchamps himself knocked on the door and when she called out for him to come in, he asked if there was anything she wanted. She nodded.

'Yes, I'd like to talk with *you*, M'sieur Duchamps, about your time in the Resistance.'

'That's all a long, long time ago, young lady. Why do you want to talk about all that anyway?'

'I want to write some articles about Resistance people.'

He laughed. 'You won't be popular in Paris if you write about me. Despite my name I'm English, and de Gaulle didn't like the English.'

'I wasn't thinking of mentioning names. I just wanted background material.'

He looked at his watch. 'I'm just doing my rounds now. How about if you have a drink with me in about an hour. Come down about one o'clock and the receptionist will show you where my rooms are.'

'Thanks very much.'

She watched him as he poured out the white wine for

them. He wasn't what she had expected although she wasn't sure what she *had* expected. He was about 5′ 7″, stocky and thick-set. Balding and grey, but he gave no impression of age. His size came from his frame and from muscle. There was no fat on the man despite his tubby appearance.

As he handed her a glass he said, 'Are you a journalist?'

She nodded. 'A freelance.'

He sat down and stretched out his legs.

'What is it you want to know?'

'Could you tell me about your training?'

He leaned back his head and stared at the ceiling. He was silent for several minutes before he spoke.

'We had training on weapons, explosives, self-defence, radio, map-reading, vehicles, the German army and intelligence services ...' He looked at her, smiling. 'Do you want me to go on?'

'What were the people like who trained you? What were they?'

'On what particular things?'

'Say weapons and self-defence.'

'On self-defence it was mainly ex-Shanghai policemen and judo experts. On weapons it was army specialists and gunsmiths.'

'Why gunsmiths?'

He shifted in his chair. 'Well if you're operating in enemy territory, or occupied territory, and something goes wrong with a pistol or a telescopic sight you can't go into a gunsmith's shop and ask for it to be repaired. You've got to be able to do it yourself.'

'Were you good with guns?'

He laughed. 'No. None of us were. The training was good but most of us couldn't have hit a man at twenty feet. Pistol shooting isn't as easy as it is in films and TV.'

'What kind of weapons did you have?'

'Smith & Wesson revolvers, .38s. Lugers, Berettas, all sorts of stuff. And rifles of course, Lee-Enfields mostly. Sten guns, Tommy guns, Brens. A bit of everything.'

'Did *you* kill people yourself?'

The small grey eyes looked at her and they were very cold. 'I wouldn't answer questions like that.'

'Is that the sort of training that spies get these days?'

'You mean KGB people, CIA and the like?'

'Yes.'

'No. In those days we used what was to hand. Nowadays the training and weapons are much more sophisticated. You'd have much tougher self-defence. Kung-fu rather than Judo.'

'You were SOE weren't you?'

'Yes.'

'Were there any women in SOE?'

'Oh yes. A lot. They were first-class.'

'What sort of things did they do? Just the paperwork?'

'Not at all. There were girls in the field. You must have heard of some of them. Odette, Violette Szabo, Paulette. Many of them were sent to camps and killed.'

'And they operated in the field the same way as men?'

'Better in some cases.'

'They were brave?'

'Of course. Why shouldn't they be?'

'What kind of women were they?'

'Their backgrounds you mean?'

'Yes.'

'Oh, all sorts of girls. Violette Szabo worked in a haberdasher's shop. They were just typical girls. Some quiet, some extrovert. Some poor, some wealthy.'

'What made them different?'

'They were fighting something they hated. They believed in what they were doing. They had an enemy.'

'The Germans?'

'The Nazis.'

'Was there a difference?'

Duchamps sighed. 'There was a difference, but we didn't feel that way at the time.'

'I'm a German.'

43

'I guessed so.'

'How could you tell?'

'You use a German "L". It's impossible to disguise it. But you speak such good French.'

'I married a Frenchman.'

'That's the way to learn. What else do you want to know?'

'Who gives the best training these days?'

'The CIA without any doubt.'

She asked him about his time in the Marseilles area with SOE but she could feel that he wasn't going to talk much about those times. And she wasn't all that interested. She had got the leads she wanted. They talked casually about the hotel and then she left.

She slept that night without taking one of the capsules.

When she drove back to Aix next morning she had already made up her mind about what she would do.

At Aix she had drawn 30,000 francs in traveller's cheques and cash from her account at the Banque de France. She also bought a school atlas.

Pierre was standing on the patio as she drove up the winding road to the villa and for a fleeting moment it seemed like coming home.

At dinner that night she told him she was going to the United States for a few weeks. He looked surprised but was obviously pleased that she could contemplate the journey. They were drinking their coffee when he looked across at her.

'I want to ask you a silly question, girl. Don't answer if you don't want to.'

'Ask me.'

'What about your parents. Have they been told about Paul?'

'No. They haven't.'

'Do you think that's wise. They might worry about you if they heard the news from somebody else.'

'They won't worry, *beau-père*.'

He wiped his mouth unnecessarily with his napkin.

'Why not?'

She told him what had happened those years ago. His eyes looked at her face.

'That must have taken tremendous courage.'

'It sickened me. But there was nothing else to do.'

'Did Paul know about this?'

'Yes.'

'So they don't know that you are married?'

'No. I've never contacted them since.'

'You don't feel that you could forgive them because they were poor?'

'No. Never. Being poor or rich is no excuse for being cruel. And we were no poorer than most.'

'What do you feel was the cruel part?'

'He just did it, Pierre. He didn't ask me or even tell me. He didn't care what it did to me.'

'It must have made you very unhappy.'

'In a way. I swamped the unhappiness with anger.'

'After you and Paul were married he seldom came down here. A phone call if I was in Paris. Nothing more. I think he didn't want to be different from you. To have an advantage that you didn't have.'

Her lips trembled and she held up her hand. 'Don't speak about Paul, *beau-père*. Not tonight.'

'Of course. But I want you to remember that you *have* got a family. Me, and aunts and uncles, cousins and nephews, all round the world from Warsaw to Tel Aviv, Hong Kong to Toronto. Lawyers, tailors, salesmen, even a violinist. They're yours too.'

She nodded. 'Can I take something with me from Paul's room?'

He was standing up pushing back his chair as she spoke. 'Of course. What is it?'

'One of the photographs.'

He smiled as he leaned back on the back of the chair.

'The one with the pony?'

45

'No. The one in the concentration camp.'

Slowly he lowered himself back into the chair. His eyes on her face.

He said, almost inaudibly. 'My God. Why that?'

'I need it. I want to be reminded.'

His hand was shaking as he poured himself more wine. When he lifted the glass his hand was still shaking and he put the glass back untouched on the table.

He leaned forward as he looked at her. 'I ask you only one question my dear.' He paused and sighed. 'I ask only if you know what you are doing.'

She wondered if he had guessed what she intended to do. But he couldn't have. She had only just made the decision herself. But he was a shrewd man, a perceptive man. She wondered what he had in mind.

'Yes, *beau-père*. I know what I am doing.'

'This is your home, you know. This is where you will always come back to. No asking, no arranging. You just come here. If I am not here the servants will do whatever you ask. They will know where I am.' He paused. 'When are you leaving?'

'If I can get a plane, tomorrow.'

'Will you leave an address?'

'No, *beau-père*, but I shall think about you and the villa when I am lonely.'

He sat rubbing one hand on the back of the other and she knew it was some reflex from being upset.

She stood up and walked round the table. She put her arm round his bulky shoulders.

'I'll go early, Pierre. Jean-Louis can drive me to Marseilles.'

She kissed the side of his face and left him alone at the table. He didn't look up as she walked through to the hall.

Chapter Seven

The clerk turned round to point.

'All CIA records in the Library of Congress are way down that end, starting at 2914.'

She thanked him and walked down past the rows of shelving. At 2914 she stopped, and almost furtively she pulled one of the files forward and lifted the lid. There was a list of contents and dates. The file covered Jan–June 1960. She moved on a couple of rows and tried again. Those records covered only one month, March 1970.

She checked file after file until she found an index covering June 1976. Taking it to the reading table she went slowly through the documents. In many cases the names and place names had been blacked out. It was in the file covering September 1976 that she found the sort of material she was looking for.

It was the record of a Senate Investigation Committee on Intelligence, covering the dismissal of two instructors from a CIA training installation. As she slowly turned the pages she tried to understand the veiled references to operational code-names, and their implications. Place names and some personal names had been expunged with black ink, but the names of the agents were left in clear. Wiczkowski and Wallace had been given a non-training operation in New York. No warrants had been obtained, or applied for, to carry out surveillance of the United States' Ambassador to the United Nations. The methods used had been illegal, and the surveillance itself unconstitutional. The motivation for the surveillance was adjudged as personal and political. Both agents had been dismissed from the CIA after the hearing, and neither of them had been asked, or had volunteered, the name of any superior who had given them their orders.

The file was marked 'Eyes only' and she had memorized both names.

That afternoon she sat in front of the micro-film reader at the Washington Post and read carefully page after page of the issues just before and just after the 26 September 1976. She read every news page deep into October, again and again. But there was nothing.

She showed the names on her paper to the clerk at the counter and asked if he could help.

'If they're not on the index, ma'am, they just ain't there.'

'What's the index?'

He smiled. 'Just press the red button on the right until you get to the letter you're looking for. It moves on two thousand entries every time you press it. Where there's a sub-entry for a big category press the blue button. Who are these guys, politicians?'

She hesitated, and the clerk shrugged. 'You don't have to tell me, lady.'

She tried the Polish name first and found fifteen references. The eighth one was the right one. There were hundreds of Wallaces and pages of sub-entries. She worked through the cross-references for three hours but there was no reference to a CIA man in the first thirty.

She re-read the entry for Wiczkowski. A reference was made to his former CIA status when the Internal Revenue had lost a case against him for back taxes. He was now employed as a security officer at a New York bank. There had been no mention of resignation or dismissal from the CIA. She wrote down the name of the bank and the number of the last Wallace reference she had read.

Back at her hotel she checked the address of the bank from the New York telephone directory.

It took her four hours the next morning to find the CIA Wallace. The reference had been in one of the issues she had already checked and there were at least forty column-inches. It was a report of the Senate Committee's investigation, with a photograph of the Ambassador. It gave no new details and the bulk was editorial philosophizing. There was no clue to where Wallace was now, or what work he was doing.

The girl packed her bag and took a taxi to the airport and it was only then that she had noticed the monuments and buildings of Washington DC. She had programmed her mind not to notice people and places unless she had to. There were occasions when to her own peril she would physically close her eyes to carelessly dressed young men with fair hair, and babies in prams. She lost track of what day it was because it didn't matter. Men in cafés and restaurants looked at her speculatively. The wise ones saw the look in her eyes and left her alone. The foolish, who talked, no matter how amiably, wondered what they had done to earn such a look of anger from the big brown eyes. Indifference they were used to, but anger, barely controlled, they put down to women's lib or lesbianism.

On the plane to La Guardia she had a window seat, she neither ate, drank nor read. Her eyes were focused on a horizon that wasn't there.

She booked a room at the Lexington because from the tourist map it looked near the bank's address at East 72nd Street. After unpacking she went out to look at the building. At street level it was all glass and chrome. Inside, it was well lit, and she could make out a marble floor, desks, counters with grilles and a host of big indoor plants. It was a Sunday and the bank was closed.

The man in the grey uniform saw her looking around and walked over.

'Can I help you, miss?'

'I was looking for Mr Wiczkowski.'

'He's on the twelfth floor, miss. Is he expecting you?'

'No.'

'I'll see if he's available.'

She walked with him to the desk that half circled one of the massive Palladian columns, and he turned away as he dialled four numbers. He spoke for a few moments then turned to look at her.

'Who shall I say it is, miss?'

'Mam'selle Duchamps.'

For a moment he hesitated over the name and then turned back to the phone. A few seconds later he hung up and turned to her. He pointed to the far side of the foyer.

'The elevators are over there, miss. If you'll go up to the twelfth he'll see you in a few minutes. But he warned that he'd got a meeting very shortly.'

'Thank you.'

'You're welcome.'

As she got out of the elevator on the twelfth floor a man was waiting there. A big man with an attractive but ugly face. His hair was thick and black, and as he put forward his hand she saw the black hairs at his wrist. His dark eyes looked her over, openly, arrogantly, and sexually. He was smiling the smile of a man who was used to being successful with women. And she loathed him immediately.

'Miss Duchamps?'

'Yes.'

He turned and pointed. 'That's my office. Make yourself comfortable. I'll be right back.'

His name was on the door, and a title. Director of Security, the Halkin Bank Group.

The office was spacious and modern but the framed photographs gave it an old-fashioned appearance. They all featured Wiczkowski. In football gear, swinging a golf club, with boxing gloves, examining a huge fish on the deck of a boat, and several where he was shaking hands with important looking men. There was one obviously taken at a nightclub with a very pretty girl looking at him adoringly as he looked at the camera. There was a row of standard targets with all the shots clustered around and in the bull, with dates and place names.

She turned as he came back in the room, smiling as he waved her to a chair in front of his desk.

'Now. What can I do for you?'

'I'm trying to check the address of Henry Wallace. I think you know him.'

He smiled. 'D'you know Hank?'

She hesitated only for a second. 'I met him once.'

The screwed-up eyes looked at her face as if he might doubt her words.

'Where was this?'

'At a party?'

'Where?'

She shrugged. 'In Washington.'

'How long ago was this?'

'A few years back.'

'What was he doing in those days?'

'I didn't ask him and he didn't tell me, but somebody told me he was with the CIA.'

'Whose party was it?'

'It was at the French Embassy.'

She decided that the next piece of interrogation she would refuse to answer, but Wiczkowski seemed to relax. He leaned back in his chair, smiling as he looked at her face.

'You took a fancy to old Hank, did you?'

'I thought he was a very nice man. And an interesting man. That's why I want to interview him.'

'You're a journalist?'

'Yes. A freelance magazine writer.'

He looked at his watch and then back at her face. 'Have you got time for some lunch?'

'What about your meeting?'

He gave her the number one smile, the one that crinkled his eyes. 'I'll always miss meetings for pretty girls.'

'OK. That would be nice.' She reached for her handbag and took out a shorthand notebook.

'You were going to give me Mr Wallace's location.'

He grinned. 'You drive a hard bargain. Let's have a look.' He reached for a thick black book and slowly turned the pages.

51

'Here we are. H. Wallace. The Sports Store, Lantenengo Street, Stanton Falls, Texas. There's no telephone number but you can check that out with the phone company.' He threw the book on one side. 'Let's eat, honey.' And he shoved back his chair and walked round the desk.

He took her to a small French restaurant where he was obviously well-known, and the table for two was as secluded as a corner and dim lights could make it.

Eating with him was a small price to pay, despite the hand under the table that slowly massaged her thigh. He talked about Hank Wallace, and guardedly of their dismissal from the CIA. According to Wiczkowski they had both been thrown to the wolves to protect people who were higher up, but their silence had earned them suitable rewards in cash payments and pensions. Wallace now had a prosperous business and Wiczkowski earned four times as much as his CIA pay. But most of the time Wiczkowski was selling himself. Blatantly but not energetically. Name and status dropping laced with none-too subtle flattery. He was used to pretty girls but a pretty girl with character and brains was what he had set his mind on. Not, she noted his heart.

She had agreed to see him the next morning, aware of his smug satisfaction as he waved down a cab for her.

Just before midnight the plane touched down at Dallas and she took a cab to the Sheraton on Main Street.

As she lay exhausted in bed, a mad, disjointed film clattered behind her closed eyes. A staircase, Wiczkowski's huge shoulders as he waved for a cab, a close up of yellow mimosa, the bank entrance at Aix, the swinging white light in the hospital, and a red tie fluttering in the wind. She lay with her legs drawn up, her hands together between her knees like some illustration for a Freudian case-history.

Chapter Eight

She checked in at the motel and they gave her directions to Lantenengo Street.

Stanton Falls lies to the north of Dallas near the Oklahoma stateline. There will be Americans who have never heard of Stanton Falls. Even Texans. The population at the last count had been just over 30,000 but it was the county seat and it served a rural area that could muster 170,000 on high days and holidays. Its founders had set it on the intersection of what was now State Highway 82 and an unnumbered road that came off 677. Its oil had been tapped rather late in the game, much to the town's advantage. The locals had not sold out to the experts, and nobody had bought 90% of the equity for the 500 dollars it took to break through the last 150 feet of rock and shale. The money had been cattlemen's money, and most of it had stayed right there in Stanton Falls. There were millionaires in Stanton Falls who drove trucks instead of cars, reconditioned trucks at that. And only two of them had ever crossed the Texas stateline.

It was a wealthy community, but extravagance didn't go much beyond a touch of marble in a bathroom or a foreign sports car. The town sat snugly between the half-circle of high hills to the north and the river to the south. The original main road is still the principal highway but time has added four parallel roads and a couple of dozen intersections. Lantenengo Street was the most westerly of these. The Sports Store spread between a dry-cleaner's and a café. They all had an air of prosperity.

She parked her hired Hertz car at the corner of the block and walked down. There was music from the café, a man with a guitar mourning the demise of his faithful friend. A dog or maybe a horse, she couldn't make out which. The sidewalk shimmered in the hot sun and her denim shirt stuck to her back. Instinct had told her since she had left Aix, never to hesitate, never to weigh up the odds. When she knew the next move she should get on and make it.

Inside the shop the air-conditioning was a relief. Her eyes took in the layout. It was bigger than she expected and more modern. In display cases there were guns and pistols, rows of sports clothes, fishing tackle, footballs, and shelves of shoes. A boy and a girl were laughing with a young assistant as the girl made tentative swings with a tennis racket. Then seeing her, the assistant had walked over. He was about 18, blue-eyed, fair-haired, tall and gangling. His smile was friendly.

'Can I help you, ma'am?'

'I'd like to speak to Mr Wallace.'

He grinned. 'My name's Wallace, but I guess you want my father.'

'Hank Wallace?'

'That's him. He's next door at the café. I'll have him out for you.'

'I don't want to disturb him.'

He laughed. 'I do. It's time he was back.'

The man who came back with the boy was exactly like him. Except for his face. The same fair hair, the same blue eyes, the same neat nose. But it was a closed-in face, the mouth unsmiling, the blue eyes non-committal.

'Hank Wallace, ma'am, can I help you?'

'I'm a journalist, Mr Wallace. I wondered if you could spare me a little of your time.'

'For what?'

'To talk. I'd like to interview you.'

'About what?'

'About the problems of converting from your CIA job to this.'

'Are you a Canadian?'

'Should I be?'

54

'You've got a French accent.'

'I am French.'

He seemed to relax a little and nodded towards the far end of the shop. 'Let's go in my office. It's a bit small but there's room for two.'

As he opened the door for her he said, 'You like a drink? A coke or a lager or something?'

'A coke would be nice.'

He stood with his back to her as he searched in a small refrigerator and then poured a coke into a plastic mug.

'Sorry about the cup. I guess Joe and I are a bit primitive.'

He waved her to a chair and pulled up another behind his small desk. She noticed that his eyes went over her with the same arrogance as Wiczkowski's. But she minded less because he had looked at her hands longer than he looked at her legs.

'I'm a freelance, Mr Wallace.'

'Is that so.'

'I'm not sure whether it will all end up as a magazine piece or a book.'

He nodded but said nothing.

'How much time could you give me?'

He looked at his watch. 'An hour, maybe a little longer. I've got a salesman due to see me at three.'

'Maybe it would be more convenient if I saw you outside working hours?'

'Let's see how it goes.'

'I read in a newspaper that you were an instructor at a CIA training establishment. Could you tell me something about that?'

He laughed, and for the first time his mouth wasn't grim, and she noticed that his eyes were a very pale blue against his tanned face.

'Lady, you must know that that kind of material is highly classified.'

'Is there any part of that we could discuss?'

'Like what?'

'How you teach people to shoot. About weapons. How to defend themselves.'

'But that's routine stuff. The US Marines could tell you all that.'

'Does that mean you won't tell me?'

'No. But why d'you pick on me?'

'I saw in the newspaper that you left the CIA and I'm more interested in that than the US Marines.'

'Why. What's wrong with the Marines?'

'Nothing. But the public are more interested in the CIA. It's more glamorous.'

The pale blue eyes looked at her sceptically.

'Do you know anything about weapons?'

'No. Nothing at all. But I'd pay you to teach me.'

His eyebrows went up and he pursued his lips. 'That would cost a pretty dollar. It couldn't be worth it. Just for writing a book.'

'It would be for me.'

'How did you trace where I live?'

'I got in touch with Mr Wiczkowski. He gave me your address.'

He smiled. 'And you survived?'

'He's no problem as long as you don't inhale.'

He laughed and stood up. 'Where are you staying?'

'At the motel on Elm Tree.'

'How long for?'

'Until you've taught me what I want to know.'

He leaned forward, his hands gripping the back of the chair. His eyes on her face.

'You know, there's something odd about you.'

'What is it?'

'You strike me as being a very honest person, and yet somehow I'm getting negative vibes. Did Buckley send you?'

'Nobody sent me. And I don't know anyone named Buckley.'

He looked at her without speaking for long moments. Then, 'What's your name?'

'Duchamps. Anna Duchamps.'

'Let me think about it. I'll call you at six this evening if that's OK with you.'

'That's fine.'

He stood watching her from the back of the store as she walked to the door. He noticed his son open the door for her and stand talking with her for a few moments.

He phoned her promptly at six and agreed to give her some basic training on weapons. She would pay the same tuition rate that his clients paid for coaching in game-shooting or target-shooting techniques. Five hundred dollars a week. He thought she would certainly need two weeks. They would start the next day, and he would call for her at the motel at 7.30 so that they could get to the range before the heat of the day had set in.

He unloaded the plywood box from the trunk of the car and carried it into the empty clubhouse. She watched as he laid out several guns on a piece of green baize. He turned to her.

'Do you know anything at all about weapons?'

'Nothing at all.'

'Right. Now because of the time factor we can't afford to go over all the instruction you would get on guns if you were trained as a marksman in any of the services or the police. But these are typical good guns . . .'

'Can I ask questions as we go along?'

He laughed. 'In the services you can't, you'd get your ear chewed off. But fire away.'

'What makes a gun a good gun?'

'A good gun does its job accurately, consistently and effectively. Let's look at these. This one in its case is a Browning Hi-power 9mm automatic. Too heavy for you to use. This is a Smith & Wesson .38 Chief's Special, a belly-gun really, a defensive weapon. Does what it says. This one here is a Luger, a .22 for target shooting. This last gun is a revolver with special contour-built grips to suit its owner's hand.

'Any questions?'

'The belly-gun. What does that do?'

'It's small, short barrelled, not accurate over a distance, but shoved in a back or a belly it does the trick.'

'Why are some called revolvers and some called pistols?'

'The Chief's Special is a revolver. This cylinder turns round as the trigger is pulled to present a new cartridge to the firing-pin. The guns without cylinders are pistols.'

He bent down, opened the lid of the wooden box and brought out another pistol. He put it on its own square of baize.

'Now,' he said. 'We are pretending that you are a new CIA agent, on a weapons course at ... on a weapons course. If you are a lightly built man or woman this is the handgun you'd be trained on. It's German made. It's called the Walther PPK. The PPK stands for Polizei Pistol-Kriminal. It's small, the barrel is under four inches, it weighs about twenty-three ounces. It's flat, no bulges, and easy to conceal. Some experts criticize it because it has a number of pressed steel parts. The agency view is that as it's not a target gun that's of no consequence. It probably won't be fired more than sixty times a year, apart from training. Pick it up and hold it.'

The girl picked it up and her hand slid round the stock. She put her arm out straight and closed one eye.

'OK, put it down.'

She put the gun back on the baize. He pressed the magazine catch and eased out the magazine. He loaded it slowly as she watched and then slid the magazine up into the stock. He checked the safety-catch and said, 'Right. Let's go on to the range.'

He put up a standard American 25 yard target and called her over.

'This is a 25 yard target, but you're going to fire from five yards.'

He paced out the distance and she stood beside him.

'Here's the pistol. The safety catch is off, fire eight shots at the target in your own time.'

She straightened her arm, closed one eye and after a few seconds she pulled the trigger. The slug whirred off into the distance. When she had fired the eight times he walked her to the target. It was untouched.

'In four days' time you'll have two shots *somewhere* on the card. At the end of the week you'll have four on the card. When we're finished they'll all be on the card – somewhere. Let's go back in the clubhouse.'

They sat alongside each other in the bamboo chairs.

'Now, when you go out there again, I want you to remember these things. No matter what anybody says, me or anybody else, you check the safety catch yourself – always – it's your responsibility. Next, don't put your arm out straight. You may be firing at a target but that's not how you would use the gun in your job. And your arm out straight can't carry the gun and hold it steady. And lastly, you've got to grip the stock hard. As if you were trying to crush it. Understood?'

'Yes.'

'Now we'll have a drink and then we'll strip that gun down. By the time you've finished your training you'll be able to assemble it blindfold.'

He went behind the bar-counter and poured them each a coke from the refrigerator. She sat on the bar stool, and he leaned on the counter.

'This afternoon I'll take you out plinking.'

'What's that?'

'Firing at cans, trees, logs, something that isn't a target card. How's the motel?'

'OK.'

'What did you do last night?'

'Had dinner and went to bed.'

He looked at her face as he sipped his drink.

'How about you eat with Tom and me tonight?'

'Is Tom your son?'

'Yep.'

'Will your wife mind?'

'I don't have a wife. She lit out way back. My sister looks after us. I'm divorced.'

'I'm sorry.'

'Don't be sorry, lady. I was glad when she left.'

'Do you ever hear from her?'

'*From* her – no. *Of* her – yes. She's what they call a hostess in a night-club in El Paso. She likes her men dark and handsome.'

There was an awkward silence and then he banged down his glass.

'OK. The pistol's empty. I want you to go out and fire at that target thirty times as if each shot was for real. Come back in when you've done that. I'll have a little present for you when you get back. I've got to phone the store.'

When she got back he was still behind the bar.

'Come on over.'

She arranged herself on the stool.

'Give me the pistol.'

He checked that the safety catch was on. 'Good girl. Now open your right hand and put it on the counter palm up.'

He saw the raw red criss-cross pattern from the walnut stock where she had gripped it tightly. He looked up at her face. 'You're really trying aren't you?'

'Yes.'

He fished in his jacket pocket. 'These are for you.' It was a pair of hand spring-grips. 'When you haven't got that pistol in your hand I want you to be squeezing that grip.'

Then he reloaded the PPK and took her out to the range. At twenty-five yards from the target he stopped and raised the gun.

'Now watch this. My shoulder's pointing at the target, my feet are properly braced.' He fired four shots. 'Now that

60

stance is fine for target shooting but that isn't why agents have guns. So here we go. Square to the target. Aim low and bend at the elbow.' He fired three more shots. 'OK,' he said. 'How many more shots to come?'

She blushed. 'I don't know. I didn't count.'

'Well let's have a look at the target.'

There were four holes in the ten ring and three in the eight ring at two o'clock.

'You see the difference. Target stance they're all in the middle. Working stance they're way up there because my wrist moved. Now. Watch me reload.'

He stood close behind her, his hand over hers on the gun. It felt as if her hand was set in concrete.

'Now fire the eight rounds.'

She fired the eight rounds and then he said, 'Now what do you do?'

'Put on the safety.'

'Good girl. You do that, and when you walk to the target with me you hold the pistol upright against your upper-arm. Come on.'

At the target there were six holes scattered wildly. He grunted and took down the card. He fished for a ball-point pen in his pocket and then signed it. When he gave it to her it said, 'Certified target of first shoot. Miss A. Duchamps – Stanton Falls RAPC signed Henry Wallace.'

He smiled as she looked up at his face.

'Come on. We'll go plinking. Sis has put us up a hamper.'

When the car left the metalled road and hit the dirt track he drove on a few hundred yards and then pulled up.

'Stay inside while I get the canopy up.'

As he fixed the canvas canopy and unloaded things from the car she looked at the landscape. There was nothing but red rock and sand, and a few stunted trees alongside the small stream. There was a sheer cliff in the distance. And mesquite and tumbleweed rolling fitfully in the surface breeze. For a moment the madness of what she was doing seized her and she shook her head closing her eyes. His voice was gentle. 'What's the matter. Are you OK?'

'I'm all right, thank you.'

'OK. Let's eat.'

There were beef sandwiches, fresh fruit and a bowl of strawberries, and for the first time for a week she ate heartily. When she was drinking a glass of milk he said, 'You're wasting time.'

She turned, frowning, to look at him. 'How?'

'Put the glass in your left hand and use the hand grip.'

She smiled. 'They must have hated you at the training place.'

The washed-out blue eyes looked at her face. 'D'you know something?'

'No. What?'

'You just smiled for the first time since I first saw you.'

He saw her face set, and her cheeks flush, and he reached for the pistol on the blanket beside him.

'See the two rocks there like an arch. Loose off seven shots. Try hard to hit them.'

She took the gun and stood up, checked the safety to off and then stood with her legs apart. She fired four shots and saw sand flick up far beyond the stones. She heard him say, 'Down a bit,' and the last shot touched one of the rocks and whirred off into the distance.

He took the pistol from her and went over to the plywood box. As she stood watching him he found a small stone and taped it to the underside of the snout of the pistol. He handed it to her after he had reloaded the magazine.

'Try again.'

This time the first five shots hit the stones.

'The last two were short because your wrist was tired. I'll fix the back-sight to suit you tonight.'

Then for an hour he sat with her, explaining the differences that cartridge charges could make to a weapon. He made her use the hand-grip all the time he was talking.

By the time she had fired another eighty rounds she was hitting the rocks consistently, but the ball of her thumb, and her wrist, felt as if they were on fire. He had taken her hand and looked at the swelling. 'We'll get that in cold water and it'll go down quickly.' He looked up at her face. 'Would you like to give it a miss tomorrow?'

She shook her head. 'No. I'll be OK.'

He drove her back to the motel and arranged to pick her up at six.

It was Tom who called for her at six, and he apologized for his father who had had to stay behind to see a salesman from one of his suppliers.

The young man said, 'Dad says you did well today. That's high praise from him.'

'I think he was being kind.'

'He's a kind man, but not about weapons. He used to drive me crazy. There was always something you did wrong. But he said you seemed highly motivated. That's his way of saying you were busting a gut to do well.'

'He's a good teacher, he probably tailors the comments to suit the person.'

'I think maybe he was trying to make up for being suspicious of you when you first spoke to him.'

'Why should he be suspicious?'

'He thought it was maybe Mom up to her tricks, and Buckley had sent you.'

'He asked me that. Who is Buckley?'

'He's her attorney. He screws her and she uses him to harass Dad about money. He paid what the court said and they split the property. I guess she gets mad when she knows he's making out all right.'

'What sort of lady is she, Tom?'

He slowed the car and stopped. He laughed without humour. 'Mom's no lady. Nobody could accuse her of that. She's very pretty. Really pretty. She was brought up in an orphanage.' He sighed. 'It's very sad really. He tried so hard to give her security. But it wasn't possible. She needed men.

Not for sex, but just to admire her looks. They did of course, but they wanted their reward in bed.'

He turned his face to look at hers and she saw the pain in his eyes. 'It sounds crazy but she was a good woman when the bastards weren't around her. Very warm and generous. I can remember times when it was great for us all.' He sighed. 'But one man's admiration wasn't ever gonna be enough for her, and some creep would hit town, and that would be it. She'd just light out. He put up with it at first. I think he understood. But after a time you could see him closing in on himself. Just self-defence.'

'How about you. Do you ever see her?'

'Not any more. She always has some guy in tow. It was always embarrassing. For her as well as me. We'd better go or he'll be there before us.'

The house was at the far end of Lantenengo Street. Inside it was very masculine. Despite his sister there was really no trace of feminine influence. Nevertheless, it was a pleasant house. Modern, spacious, a good machine for living in.

After Wallace arrived they ate and afterwards the two men showed her how to play poker.

Wallace drove her back to the motel and as she stood outside her cabin he said, 'By the way, I had a call from Wiczkowski in New York. Said you had a date with him you hadn't kept.'

She looked up at his face. 'I'm afraid that's true. I didn't fancy him.'

He opened his mouth as if he were going to speak, and then closed it.

'What were you going to say?'

'Nothing. Seven thirty tomorrow morning OK?'

'Fine.'

'You did well today.'

'Thanks.'

He turned and she watched as he walked to the car. He didn't look back.

The girl was lying on her back, her legs threshing wildly, her fingers clawing at his hands. She felt an appalling pain behind her ear and then the sky seemed to turn on its side as she began to lose consciousness. Then the pain receded.

He helped her to her feet and supported her with his arm while she recovered. It was the tenth day of her training and she now knew the effect of even a light touch on the pressure point behind her ear. He took her thumb and slid it into the concavity behind his ear where his jaw met his skull.

'Put your other thumb on top of that thumb and use one to add pressure to the other. Good. More. STOP.' He snatched her hand away, smiling. 'I can't let you do it because you won't know when to stop. A medium pressure from one thumb will put a man out for three hours. Full pressure will kill him in two minutes, but you'd have to put all your body weight behind your thumb. Go get the pistol.'

She walked over to the box and picked up the pistol, checking the safety catch, and she carried it upright without thinking. He turned his back to her and said, 'OK. Put the gun in my back like they do in films. As hard as you like. Then tell me to walk, and keep the gun in my back.'

She jammed the pistol against his spine. 'Move forward slowly,' she said.

She didn't see what happened but suddenly the gun was in his hand, pointing at her.

'Never, never,' he said, 'put a gun or a knife against a man. Either his back or his belly. If he knows what he's doing he'll have you in minutes. Keep back at least four feet. I'll do it slowly.'

He turned his back to her and she pushed the gun against his back. He turned slowly and the gun slid past his body. His hands gripped her wrist and the gun dropped on the blanket.

'As soon as I'm turning the gun is past me. If you fire it, the slug can't touch me and if you try to re-aim the gun it'll take a minimum of six seconds and in that time I'll have the gun. Now we'll practise that with the gun in your back. Slowly the first few times. Then faster.'

For an hour they had worked at it. The last six times with the safety catch off. Three times he had pulled the trigger. One slug had caught her jacket, but the others had splatted into the sandbags.

'OK,' he said finally. 'That's enough for you today. I've got a surprise for you this evening.'

He saw the brown eyes light up for a moment. 'What is it? Tell me.'

She was standing close to him, he could see the beads of perspiration on her face and smell the sweat of her body. And for a second there was a look in her eyes. His mouth was on hers and his arms around her, holding her body to his. For a moment her body clung to his, her mouth responding to his. Then she cried out and pushed him away. He saw a look of revulsion on her face.

'I'm sorry, Anna. I shouldn't have done that.'

She took a deep breath and her body shivered. She said softly, 'It's all right, Hank. Forget it.'

'I won't forget it. I'm sorry I offended you.'

The brown eyes looked at his face. 'You didn't offend me, Hank. It's nothing to do with you. It's me.'

'Tell me,' he said softly, with obvious concern.

She sighed. 'I can't, Hank.'

He took her hand and walked over to the sandbags.

'Sit down, sweetie.'

She sat beside him staring straight ahead and he looked for a long time at her face. He thought again that she was very beautiful.

'You worry me, Anna.'

She turned to look at him. 'Why, Hank?'

'Can I say the truth?'

'Of course.'

'I've taught a lot of people how to shoot. Girls as well as men.

'I've never taught anyone as determined and single-

66

minded as you. Neither man nor girl. It doesn't fit in.'

'With what?'

He sighed. 'I don't believe that you're doing this just to write an article or a book.'

'So why am I doing it?'

'I don't know. That's what worries me.'

'Don't get involved with me, Hank.'

'I'd like to be involved. I'm . . . fond of you.'

She smiled. 'After only six days.'

'After only two.'

'How? Why?'

'I don't know. I just feel you need taking care of.'

'Not another lame dog, Hank. One of those in a lifetime is more than enough.'

'I don't see you that way.'

The big brown eyes looked at his face for several moments before she spoke.

'Would it help if I slept with you tonight, Hank?'

She saw the genuine surprise in his eyes and then he looked down at her hand on a sandbag. Then back at her face.

'Whatever I say will be wrong, honey. Yes, I'd love to sleep with you tonight. But no, it wouldn't help. I genuinely wasn't thinking in those terms. Like any other man I'm aware that you're beautiful and desirable. And I ain't no saint. I'd be happy to settle for holding your hand and a good-night kiss when you're feeling pleased with the world.'

She put her hand on his very gently, and she spoke very gently. 'I like you, Hank. You're a good man, and I feel very safe with you. I'd like to leave it like that.'

'Is there somebody else?'

For a moment she opened her mouth to say no but it seemed as if she would be denying Paul. And suddenly she couldn't speak. She just looked at him and he saw the tears at the edge of her eyes. He looked away, took her hand and stood up.

'Let's get back. And I'll pick you up as usual at six.'

67

After they had eaten and the dinner things had been cleared away Hank Wallace disappeared for a few moments and came back with a parcel. It was gift-wrapped and he laid it on the table in front of her. For a moment she closed her eyes to fight back the nausea and the vision of fair hair and a red tie fluttering in the wind, and her hands were shaking as she opened the package. The PPK lay there, but its standard stocks had gone. They had been changed for customed stocks to fit her hand.

She picked up the pistol, checked the safety, and closed her hand round the walnut stocks. The gun fitted as if it were part of her hand. She looked up at him. 'This is why you made me hold the piece of clay.'

He smiled. 'Yes. And the extra weight on the thumbrest will counter your tendency to fire high. Look at the trigger.'

She turned the gun on its side. On the trigger was a small shield-like device. She looked up at him. 'What is it, Hank?'

'It's called a trigger-shoe. It gives your finger more area to work against. It will feel like you don't have to squeeze so hard. I'm taking you down to an Army range in Fort Worth tomorrow and you'll be shooting moving targets.'

'I hope I don't let you down.'

'If you fire badly it'll be my inadequate training.'

She smiled at him. 'Don't kid me.'

The pale blue eyes looked back at her. 'You smiled.'

He stood reading from the paper on his clip-board.

'Moving Colt silhouette at ten yards. First shoot, one K, four Ds. Second shoot, three Ks, four Ds. Third shoot, two Ks, three Ds.'

'What are Ks and Ds?'

'Ks are killing shots. Ds are disabling shots. If you were a cop you would have qualified as a marksman. We'll have a coke and then I want you to fire another forty rounds.'

Early on the Sunday morning she drove back to Dallas. Hank Wallace had driven behind her until just before the lead road to the Highway. She had waved as she saw him stop and flash his lights, and then she was alone. She knew that she would miss Hank Wallace and his small family. In different circumstances she could have been tempted to see what happened if she stayed on for a few weeks. But that would have had to have been before she met Paul. It was like comparing a farm-horse with a race-horse. He had the same patience as Paul and that ability to teach. And in some ways more experience of the world than Paul. Nothing would ever surprise him. Despite his easy-going air there was a tension, a permanent awareness, like a hunting animal. There would be plenty of women who would fancy Hank Wallace as husband or lover. She remembered his strong hand clamped round hers on the gun as he showed her how to aim. She guessed he must be at least forty, maybe a few years more, but his alertness and toughness made him seem much younger.

She switched on the radio. It was Charles Trenet singing, 'La Mer' and Hank Wallace was suddenly a long way away.

Chapter Nine

O'Hare may be the United States' busiest airport, but it would take no prizes for architecture or creature comforts. Maybe that's why it's so busy

She found a telephone and dialled the Chicago Tourist Bureau. They gave her the addresses of two motels in Naperville and she took a cab. She chose the second address because it had easy access to the East-West Tollway.

The room was sparsely furnished but clean, and she sat on the bed looking at the street map that covered Aurora. According to the local telephone directory, Jansen's place was on one of the main roads with its stores depot out of town, on the road to Naperville.

She looked at her watch. It was too late to do anything that day. She phoned a local car rental company and asked for a car to be delivered the next morning at ten.

Jansen's place had a big sign across the front of the showrooms – Liberty Builders Inc. The stores depot was five miles back on the highway. A vast area of stores and sheds enclosed behind an eight foot barbed-wire fence, and warnings that guard dogs were on patrol day and night. There were great stacks of bricks and stone, covered along the top with tarpaulin.

In the showroom windows there were architects' impressions of houses on display boards, and a girl at a desk with a typewriter and a switchboard.

Two blocks further on there was a real-estate dealer and as she walked inside, a middle-aged man got up from a small desk.

'G'morning miss, what can I do for you?'

'Good morning. We're moving down here in six months time. We're thinking of building and I wondered if you had any building plots available.'

He pulled out a chair for her and sat on the edge of his desk.

'We've got several good plots. Where have you got in mind?'

'Well my husband will be working at the National Accelerator Laboratory, so let's say a fifteen mile radius from there.'

'That's fine. Let me show you what we've got on the books.'

She listened with interest as he showed her drawings and photographs of three possible sites. When he had finished she said, 'Can I keep these details?'

'Of course.'

She stood up and put her hand to her head. 'I nearly forgot. What local builders could you recommend?'

'Well now. There's O'Malley's. They've done a lot of high-class dwelling houses. And there's Burlington's in Naperville. Both good people. I know their principals personally, and I'd be glad to introduce you.'

She frowned. 'There was a builder's showroom I noticed as I walked here.'

'Ah yes. That'll be Liberty Builders. A Mr Jansen is the principal. He's an old friend of mine. We're golfing partners from time to time.'

'Are they a good company?'

'Excellent. Very thorough. Fair prices. Would you like me to check if he's in, and I could take you down and introduce you?'

'Yes, certainly.'

Jansen was standing in his showroom waiting for them. He was a tall man, big built and paunchy. His face tanned and deeply lined, and his grey hair crew-cut.

When the introductions and explanations were over the real-estate man tactfully left them. Jansen showed her into his back office. There were several desks covered with rolled up plans and files.

He pulled a chair for her and leaned back himself against a filing cabinet.

'I didn't quite get your name, madam.'

'Mrs Duchamps.'

'Have you got any particular specification in mind?'

'We'll need three or four bedrooms, two reception rooms, two bathrooms. A study and all the usual bits and pieces.'

He showed her tear-sheets from magazines, a book of standard plans, and he gave her the names of two architects in case she chose to start from scratch. Then he gave her his card and walked with her to the street door.

She checked in the telephone book for his private address. It was out near a local airfield for private planes.

Late in the afternoon she visited one of the architects. He was out and not due back for half an hour, and his secretary invited her to stay. She turned their talk to Jansen. He had had an American partner when he first set up in business in 1950 but Jansen had bought him out when he became a citizen in 1958. People said that he had lived in the Argentine for a few years after the war, but she wasn't sure if that was true. He wasn't married although he was very much the ladies man, and a good catch, she thought. Not her type, she felt. Not that she'd been asked. A bit too much 'machismo' for her taste. But lots of them seemed to like it. He was over 60 and some of the girls were far too young. A lovely house and plenty of money. Voted Republican and didn't mind who knew. There had been a scandal some years back. Something to do with a city building contract for two schools. Talk of call-girls available at Jansen's house for people at County Hall in Geneva.

The architect's arrival put a stop to the flow. He was a young man and he listened carefully to her description of what she was looking for. He asked sensible questions and recommended one of the available plots as likely to be a good investment. He mentioned that he had designed Jansen's own house and she asked if she could see the design.

He walked over to a plan-chest and pulled out a drawer. After leafing through the drawings he pulled out two sheets. He laid them on a table and she stood beside him as he pointed out the features of the house. She asked him how much it had cost and he got out the original specifications and tenders. It had come out at 60,000 dollars when it had been built four years before. He estimated that it would cost 20% more at current prices. But she saw what she was looking for; 10,000 dollars for electronic security equipment.

Back at the motel she planned her next day's movements.

The next day she had driven two hundred miles, timing and measuring the distance between the various locations. In daylight and in darkness.

She had cut down the time from Jansen's house to the Tollway by ten minutes during the day, and from his depot to the Tollway by four minutes in daylight. She needed to find other routes she could use by night, but she didn't think she need bother about timings from the depot. It was getting through Naperville that was taking the time.

She woke suddenly the second night, her heart beating wildly, her mind full of a sense of fear. She found herself standing by the side of her bed. Unable to think where she was. The country, the town wouldn't come to her mind. No possibilities, no names, came to her. She sank back on to the bed, her head in her hands, trying desperately to recall what was happening. Rain was beating on the windows and she looked up and saw lightning flash behind the curtains. And she remembered with a flood of depression where she was. She walked slowly over to the dressing-table and opening her handbag took out the photograph. She stood staring at it as her hand picked up the bottle of capsules. Slowly she walked back to the bed, and sat down, propping the photograph against the table lamp at the side of her bed. She shook out two of the blue/green sleeping pills and swallowed them without water. She lay back on the bed, her head turned to look at the photograph until the pill took effect and her eyes closed.

Chapter Ten

After two weeks she knew the area thoroughly. Her driving time from Jansen's house to the Tollway had been cut to the minimum. Every day she checked the PPK and loaded and unloaded the cartridges from the chamber. She used the hand-grips until her right hand was calloused, and the long tendon on her forearm was almost too noticeable. And every day she looked at the grim photograph.

The fit of depression that had overcome her the one night had acted as a catalyst. A dividing line between one life and another. This would be her life now, until she had done what she set out to do. Nothing else mattered. There would be no doubts and no fears. There was nothing to lose.

During the two weeks she had visited various stores looking at domestic appliances and furniture, and checking out the available rented accommodation.

Jansen had phoned her several times in the first week to inquire if she had decided on a plot or the house design. By the second week he had become her unofficial adviser, driving her round Aurora pointing out the places of interest and introducing her to various local worthies. She turned down his offer to teach her to play golf but accepted two invitations to dinner parties at his house. The guests were all leading businessmen and their wives and the conversation was devoted to talk of discounts and cost-effectiveness, laced with some heavy gallantries to herself and the other ladies. Despite his obvious wealth and success Jansen was still the old-fashioned German. In speech and outward show he was more American than any American but for her the German background showed

75

through. He was like her father would have been if he had been successful.

After both dinner parties Jansen had driven her back to her motel. The second time he had obviously decided that he could go a little further than amiability.

'How long before your husband joins you, honey?'

'Oh, about six or seven weeks.'

'Why stay in a dump like this? Why not let me fix you up in one of my apartments. You could make yourself really at home.'

'That would be far too expensive, Mr Jansen.'

'Not *Mr* Jansen, for heaven's sake. Ludy's my name with friends.' His arm went round her shoulder. 'Don't worry about money, kid. We could make some arrangements that suited us both.'

'I'll think about it.'

'Good girl.' And his mouth was on her and his hand slid down to cover her breast. Tense and revolted she released herself gently but firmly. She smiled up at him.

'Don't forget I'm a married girl, Ludy.'

He laughed. 'They're the ones who know what it's all about.'

'You're being very naughty, Mr Jansen.'

'I've got the Mayor and his wife coming for dinner on Sunday, how about you make up the foursome.'

'OK. What time?'

'I'll pick you up myself about seven-thirty.'

'Fine.'

And as she opened the door he playfully smacked her bottom.

'Be good, honey. Till Sunday.'

In her room at the motel she knew that there was no point in waiting much longer. Jansen was completely without suspicion. He knew nothing about her, his arrogance and self-importance made it so easy. To him she was just a girl who, with a little effort on his part, might spread her legs for him. Even his lust was casual, she wasn't special so

76

far as he was concerned. It was part of his ritual. The dominant stag gathering another stray hind to his fold. She had given no thought to what the four ODESSA men would be like. She didn't care what they were like, but Jansen, now that she had seen him and experienced him exactly represented what she would naturally loathe. He fitted the ODESSA role perfectly. Visions of concentration camp victims would never haunt Jansen's dreams and the killing of a French Jew would be no more than a minor administrative problem. A few phone calls, a brief meeting and some money and then he could get back to important things like building a swimming pool or having a girl.

On the Sunday evening after his other two guests had left, Jansen had put on a cassette. The wine had been a heavy red Bordeaux and he had been meticulous in keeping her glass topped up. As he listened to the soft sweet music he loosened his tie and took off his jacket throwing it on to a chair. He was humming softly as Sinatra sang 'My Way', and his bulky figure looked faintly ridiculous as he silently mouthed the words and mimed Sinatra's gestures.

Then his hand reached out and touched a switch on the elaborate wall-panel and as the lights slowly dimmed he held out his arms to her, inviting her to dance. He held her in his arms as the music changed to a lush waltz.

He made no attempt to hold her tightly but she could feel his hardness against her belly. But a few moments later he pulled her to him, and his mouth was on hers. When the movement of his body was overtly sexual she gently pushed him away. 'Not now, Ludy. Not now.'

'When?' he said hoarsely. 'When shall it be?'

She looked up at his face and saw the lust in his eyes. 'Tomorrow, maybe.'

'Come to dinner. Just you and me.'

His strong arm pulled her against him again.

'And then we'll do it, yes?'

She smiled up at him, and said softly, 'Yes. We'll do it then.'

She sat on the bed checking her list as if it were a list of household chores. She had paid another week's rent to the motel and told them she would be away for two days. Her bags were packed and in the hired car. The Air Canada open ticket to Toronto was in her handbag with her passport.

At four in the afternoon she had driven the car to Phillips Park and left it parked and locked in a small avenue near the intersection where Jansen's home backed on to the park. She had walked through the park and then taken a cab back to the motel.

Jansen had called for her at the motel at exactly eight o'clock. Amiable and jocular, he disguised the anticipation in his eyes, with a stream of descriptions of the day's doings at Liberty Builders Inc.

At the house there was no sign of the two servants and the meal was already laid out. A cold buffet with soup on a warming plate.

He served the food himself and the music on the hi-fi was soft and romantic.

Not too subtly he laid out the advantages for his favoured friends of his wealth and influence. And his eyes furtively looked at her body and with open admiration at her face.

He poured coffee from a percolator and after lighting a cigar he looked across at her.

'I expect you know that you're beautiful?'

She smiled. 'Pleasant rather than beautiful, Ludy.'

'Not in my book, Anna. If you were mine you wouldn't be roaming around on your own.'

'What should I be doing, Ludy?'

He smiled, and leaned forward. 'I'll show you later, sweetie.'

'I shall look forward to that.'

He stubbed his cigar in the remains of a bowl of fruit salad. 'How old are you, Anna?'

'Twenty-seven, nearly twenty-eight.'

'The perfect age.'

'Perfect for what?'

'Let's go, and I'll show you.'

'Where are Ramon and the girl?'

He smiled. 'They're out for the evening, my love. I'm very discreet.'

'I've got something to show you, Ludy.'

His eyes twinkled. 'I know, my dear. I can't wait to see it.'

'Something before that.'

She reached down beside her chair for her handbag, brought it up to her lap under the table. she opened it and her right hand closed tight round the familiar stock of the gun and her left hand slid out the photograph. She glanced down at it and then put it up on the table, turning it to face him. He was smiling, happy to humour a pretty girl. As he craned forward to look at the picture she said softly, 'D'you remember those days, Herr Sturmbanführer?'

The smile faded as he looked at the photograph and slowly his head came up to look at her face. His eyes full of disbelief.

'What the hell is this, Anna?'

And then he saw the gun in her hand and he reached across the table. 'You stupid bitch, you . . .'

Her finger squeezed the trigger and as the detonation rang around the room she saw Jansen stagger back, his chair falling behind him and then his body seemed to collapse in slow motion, his eyes staring, his mouth open as his knees bent. And then the dinner plates and glasses jumped and rattled as his body hit the floor. For a few moments that seemed like hours she just sat there, the gun in her hand, the explosion still ringing in her ears.

She stood up slowly, pushed back her chair and walked round the table to where Jansen lay with one arm outspread and the other across his face as if he were shielding it from the sun. She bent down and looked at the white shirt. There was no blood, just a tear in the thin material on his chest. She

79

unbuttoned the shirt and pulled it aside. There was just a small puncture, white with a blue encircling ring of frayed flesh. Her left hand reached for his wrist. She searched for a pulse but there was none. She tugged to turn his body and it rolled easily and a great gush of blood flooded from the open gash in his back. The whole of the back of his shirt was soaked in blood.

After walking back to the table she slid the photograph and the pistol into her handbag and walked into the hallway to get her coat. As she walked towards the door, her coat over her arm she remembered the electronics and walked back into the dining-room towards the open french windows that gave on to the patio. As she looked up at the sky she cursed softly in German and walked back into the room. She found the empty shell-case ten feet from the table under one of the chairs and slipped it into her pocket.

Walking out briskly onto the patio she didn't even glance at Jansen's body. Her mind was on the parked car.

Chapter Eleven

She was still asleep as the plane started the final descent and she woke only when the landing wheels touched the tarmac and the engines went into reverse. The streets of Toronto were deserted in the early morning darkness, a tanker was spraying water to lay the dust on Bay Street, and a yellow Metro patrol car cruised slowly by, its red light flashing. The cab dropped her at the entrance to the Sutton Place Hotel, and a porter carried her bags into the empty, silent foyer. The night clerk booked her in and the porter took her up to her room.

She sat at the dressing-table brushing her hair, listening to an all-night phone-in on the radio. The callers aired their views on abortion, capital punishment, politicians and dog-owners. The news on the hour announced the break-down of the SALT talks in Vienna, that a meeting of OPEC in Venezuela had decided to raise the price of oil as a counter to the US government's new oil quotas, and confirmed a report that a Soviet trawler had been arrested for fishing in Canadian territorial waters. There was a serious warehouse fire still out of control in Montreal and a two-day strike at Island Ferries. It was going to be another hot day with showers by mid-evening.

She sat on the bed with one leg bent under her, looking at the street map of Amsterdam in the Fodor guide-book.

The weather forecast had said sunshine until mid-afternoon and the business commuters looked annoyed at the early morning shower.

She sat reading the *Sun* at her table in the Coffee Shop. The Montreal Canadians had closed out the Stanley Cup series by beating the Maple Leaves the previous evening.

There was gossip that Premier Trudeau and his wandering wife might have effected a reconciliation. Unemployment in Newfoundland and Nova Scotia had reached an all-time high. There was little news from the United States and none from Chicago. The province of Ontario seemed to have problems enough of its own.

When the shower was over she walked across the block to Yonge Street and slowly checked the shop windows. It was half an hour before she saw what she wanted. The shop window framed a display of used sewing machines, type-writers, radios and minor office machines.

The shopkeeper lifted the two portables from the window, opened their cases and offered her paper so that she could try the two machines.

She bought the heavier of the two and took it back to the hotel. It was a second-hand Olivetti manual, its pale blue case scuffed bare at the corners. The only tools that she bought were a screw driver and a file. She also bought a chamois cleaning leather and glue at a DIY shop.

It took her two days to make the adjustments and then she booked a flight to Shannon for that night, and an onward flight to Amsterdam. The plane surged through the darkness and she slept with her feet on the typewriter, a blanket over her legs. The flight had taken off at midnight, Toronto time, and it was one o'clock in the morning, local time, when they landed at Shannon. There were two hours to wait before the Amsterdam flight left.

They gave her a tourist guide and street-map of Amsterdam at the KLM desk and she sat in the restaurant drinking coffee as she re-checked the street layout. It was going to be more difficult this time; Hans Stein's place was right in the centre of the town.

'Will passengers for KLM flight 904 to Amsterdam please go to Gate 4.'

With her coat over her arm she walked to Gate 4 and

stood in the queue for her boarding card to be checked. The ground hostess smiled at her. 'Have a nice journey.'

She stood waiting for the security check. There were two men at a low bench and a girl with a metal-detector at a temporary barrier. When she was called she put her coat, handbag and typewriter on the bench. The security guard squeezed the pockets of her coat and put it to one side. As he opened her handbag he said, 'Open the typewriter please.' He checked the bag carefully, glanced at the typewriter, snapped the lid back in place and pointed to the girl with the detector. She collected her stuff from another table after she had gone through the barrier, and followed the other passengers down the corridor.

There was no security check for transit passengers at Shannon and none at Schiphol.

She walked down the Damrak to the Royal Palace, across the Square to Raadhuisstraat where she turned right into Keizersgracht.

The house was narrow, beautifully proportioned; four storeyed with a bell gable and a hoisting beam with a white-painted hook. The façade was reddish-brown brick with stone window frames and an elaborately carved crest marking the date when the house had been built – 1637. Four steps led up from the cobbled street, flanked by wrought-iron railings. Net curtains covered the big street-level windows, and on a brass plate was the legend – Kunsthuis Stein. A typewritten sheet hanging inside the nearest window announced a private concert of the Nieuw Kammermuziek Vereen at 8.30 p.m. that evening. The programme would include songs by Rachmaninov, a Chopin piano sonata, a Schubert trio and an unaccompanied cello partita by a local composer.

A young man in blue denims, carrying a violin case smiled at her as they walked up the steps together. He spoke to her in Dutch and she shrugged and replied in German. Like any good Amsterdamer he slipped into German as if it were his own mother-tongue.

'It's a prompt start tonight because of the Schubert. You all get real value tonight.'

'Do I have to be a member?'

'I think either a member or the guest of a member. Who do you know?'

'I don't know anybody, I just saw the notice.'

He half-bowed, smiling. 'Be my guest, but you'll have to pay your own three guilders. I'm broke, as always.'

She paid the plump, smiling woman sitting at the green baize card-table and was given a duplicated programme.

Sitting in one of the comfortable tapestry chairs in the third row she looked cautiously around. There were about thirty people altogether. The concert was taking place in the main room of the gallery, a beautiful room with Palladian pillars, pale green walls framed in white wood, and touched at the corner carvings with gilt. A Blüthner baby grand stood with its lid open, flanked by gilt stools and music stands. There were small groups of members talking and laughing and she saw the young violinist talking to a tall elegant man in a plum-red velvet suit. The tall man looked across at her and then walked, smiling, towards her, his hand held out.

'Good evening. Jan says you speak German, so I take the liberty of speaking German too. Hans Stein. This is my gallery and welcome to our small gathering. Where are you from?'

'Berlin.'

'Are you on holiday in Amsterdam?'

'Part holiday, part business.'

'Wonderful. And you like chamber-music?'

'Of course.'

He smiled, nodding his approval. 'Perhaps when the concert is over I could show you round the gallery?'

'That would be very nice, Herr Stein.'

The soft, brown eyes looked at her face. 'You remember

names very well, madame. But I must get us started.' He bowed and almost imperceptibly clicked his heels. It was Wehrmacht rather than SS.

She was surprised when Stein sat down at the piano and accompanied the tenor in the two Rachmaninov songs, and his playing was outstanding but unobtrusive. There were no histrionic gestures and as she watched his face and hands she found it disturbing that he was not what she had expected. There was no grey in his black wavy hair and for a man who must be sixty or more he looked surprisingly young. She realized too that he was good-looking, and only the lines each side of his mouth gave any hint of harshness. There was a long, narrow white scar that ran from just below his chin across his neck, and the whiteness stood out against his dark skin. This was no Ludwig Jansen, and she realized that it had been a mistake to imagine them all as typical Nazis; tough, crude thugs. For a moment she wondered if the Centre in Vienna could have made a mistake. This man looked a civilized man, a cultured man; not an ex-Gestapo man. Was it possible to brutalize women and children and play Rachmaninov as this man did, with tenderness and feeling?

She was barely aware of the rest of the music before the interval and she had to force herself to come back to the present when the violinist and Stein each brought her a glass of white wine. They grinned at each other as they both proffered her a glass. Stein bowed and laughed. 'Your devoted servants, ma'am.'

When she took both glasses Stein had turned to the young man and said, 'Pieter was up to his old games again in the Schubert.'

The Dutchman smiled at the girl. 'Pieter was the cellist in the Schubert trio. He loves it so much he hangs on to his notes and drives the other two crazy.' He laughed and looked at Stein. 'He does it out of love, Hans, and love makes better music than precision.'

Stein raised his eyebrows, pouting his doubt. 'Maybe, my friend, but the music is the music after all.'

85

The young man looked at the girl, laughing. 'You Germans, always sticking to the instructions on the tin.'

She saw the flash of anger under Stein's dark skin. But he was too urbane a man to take open umbrage. He sighed. 'It's a good job some of us stick to the rules.'

Then there was the Chopin. And that too was played by Stein. It was the Sonata in B flat minor with all its poetry intact. She wondered how Stein had felt when he was a Gestapo officer in Poland, wiping out the composer's countrymen. Did he do it because an order was an order. Sticking to the rules. Or did he do it blindly and with lust. She shook her head involuntarily to dismiss the scenario in her mind, and the woman sitting next to her looked quickly at her face. When Stein played the exquisite middle section of the slow movement she closed her eyes so that she could avoid looking at him. Against her will she found herself applauding when the last notes died away.

When the concert was over the young Dutchman had approached her. 'Can I escort you back to your hotel *mevrouw?*'

For a moment she hesitated, then she said, 'That would be very nice.'

Then Stein was there beside them both. 'Let me show you round the gallery as I promised.' He made it sound as if she had asked to be shown round.

'Jan is going to walk me home. Perhaps I could call at the gallery tomorrow?'

'Of course. Of course. How about you come around four o'clock. I'll feed you strawberries for tea.'

She walked slowly back to the hotel with the young Dutchman and he chattered away about Amsterdam, the Concertgebouw, and music in general, until they were at her hotel near the Central Station. On impulse she invited him into the lounge for a drink.

She watched him over her glass as she sipped a whisky. He was in his mid-twenties, a large ungainly young man, untidy, but unselfconscious and comfortable.

'What did you think of our Hans?' he said.

'A city charmer I should imagine.'

He laughed softly. 'Very craftily put. The word "city" works like a slow poison on the compliment.'

'Oh no.'

He laughed and looked at her face. 'Oh yes. Don't spoil a good quote.'

'You mustn't repeat it, Jan.'

'What's your name?'

'Anna. Anna Hartman.'

'Mrs or miss?'

'Mrs.'

'What a shame.'

'Why?'

'I rather like you.'

She briefly bowed her head. 'I'm flattered.'

He laughed. A comfortable, shaggy dog laugh.

'You'll enjoy the gallery actually. He's built it up from nothing to one of the leading modern galleries in the city. He's got a real eye for the new painters. Some people say he's the second or third richest art-dealer in town.'

'Is he married?'

He looked at her quickly, half frowning. 'Hans married? Couldn't you tell?'

'Tell what?'

'Our dear Hans is queer. It sticks out a mile. Just take a look at those eyes.'

'What about his eyes?'

'At the front there's those big, faithful, spaniel brown eyes, but at the back you'll sometimes see something quite evil looking out. He's a tough cookie is our Hans.'

'What did he do before he came to Amsterdam?'

'He says he was Wehrmacht. I doubt it. Looks more like SS to me.'

'Don't the Dutch people resent him?'

'No. Not really. He won' thave operated here or the security police would have turfed him out long ago. He's harmless now. Except for the little boys of course.'

'Nevertheless, he does have great charm.'

The young man grinned. 'Of course. You'll like him. All the girls do.'

'Does he live at the gallery?'

'There's an apartment on the top floor he uses during the week, but at week-ends he's generally out at his farm.'

'Where's the farm?'

'Out past the airport a few kilometres this side of Aalsmeer.'

'What does he grow?'

'Pigs, blackcurrants, and small boys.'

'What do *you* do apart from playing the violin?'

'I'm a policeman.' He laughed as he said it because he was used to the surprise on people's faces when he told them.

'I can hardly believe it.'

'Why not?'

'You look so . . . so . . .' She shrugged. '. . . so cosy.'

He put back his head and laughed. 'I must tell that to the Inspector. He always says – "a detective should blend in easily with the crowd". Cosy . . .' he said, rolling the word on his tongue. 'I like that.'

She stood up. 'It's late and I'm tired, Jan.'

'Can I see you tomorrow?'

'The day after.'

'What time?'

'You say.'

'About seven. I'll call for you.'

'Fine.'

The black Buick pulled up outside the Sports Store in Lantenengo Street, ignoring the 'No Parking' sign. And the man who got out and quietly closed the door stood looking up and down the street with his hands on his hips. He was tall and big built, with a raw, ugly face that had no redeeming features. He walked slowly across the sidewalk towards the

88

store, letting his hands fall into place as he approached the door.

Inside the store he stood patiently as Wallace demonstrated a multiplier reel to a man and two boys. His eyes noted the display cases of guns, the rear office door, and the telephone on the counter.

When the sale had been made he stood there, his arms folded as Wallace came towards him.

'Sorry to keep you waiting, sir. What can I do for you?'

The big man looked him over. 'Are you Wallace? Henry James Wallace?'

'Yes.'

'Can I have a word with you in private?'

Wallace looked surprised by the question and slightly antagonistic.

'We can talk here. I'm on my own for a bit.'

'Maybe you could close the store for half an hour or so.'

Wallace frowned his annoyance. 'No way, mister, if you want to talk, then talk here. Who are you anyway?'

'My name's Altieri. FBI.'

Wallace's blue eyes looked suspicious. 'Let me see your ID.'

Altieri slid his big hand into his top pocket, pulled out the leather bound card, opened it so that it faced Wallace, held it there for a few moments, then closed it and slid it back in his pocket.

'What's it all about, Altieri?'

'It's not for discussion out here, mister.'

For a moment Wallace hesitated, then he walked to the phone and dialled a number.

'Is Tom there, Harry? Fine, ask him to come in right away. Yes. Tell him to leave it.'

He hung up and looked through the window to the street ignoring the FBI man.

When his son pushed through the door with half a hamburger in his hand Wallace said, 'Look after the store for a bit, son. I'll be in the back office.'

'OK, Dad.' The boy looked inquiringly at Altieri but nobody made any introductions and the two men walked to the back of the store.

Inside the small office Wallace waved the FBI man to the chair, and sat, himself, behind his small desk.

'OK, Altieri, what is it?'

The FBI man's florid face turned slowly to look at Wallace.

'Why are you so defensive, my friend?'

Wallace leaned forward angrily and a paper fluttered to the floor.

'I'm a civilian now, mister. Just remember that.'

The ugly face creased slowly into a smile. 'I thought you guys always said "once a spook always a spook".'

'I never heard anyone say that in all my time with the company. You've been reading too many books.'

Altieri shrugged. 'OK, let's play it your way.'

He reached for his jacket pocket and threw a small metal object on Wallace's desk.

'When did you last see that, Wallace?'

Hank Wallace reached out and picked up the small object. It was a Henshaw trigger shoe. He looked up at Altieri.

'I guess I've seen hundreds of these in my time, mister, it's a trigger shoe.'

'Have you sold many of them?'

'Yes. Lots of them.'

'D'you keep a list of customers you sell them to?'

Wallace laughed. 'No.'

'You're supposed to. They're gun accessories.'

'Not in this State you aren't.'

'Have you got any in stock right now?'

'Yes.'

'How many?'

'Twenty, thirty maybe.'

'OK. Let's go see them.'

Altieri walked with Wallace to the glass cases, Wallace

unlocked one of the glass panels and slid it along. He sorted through the small cardboard boxes, lifted one out, and turned to put it on the counter.

The FBI man took off the cover and looked inside. After a few moment he slid back the lid, picked up the box and walked back to Wallace's office.

'I'll take charge of these and give you a receipt.'

'Have you got a warrant of any kind?'

'Nope.'

'Well you just put that damn box down until you have.'

Altieri sighed. 'It won't take me twenty minutes to get a warrant, my friend, but you won't like the charge that goes with it.'

Wallace snorted. 'Selling trigger shoes without keeping a record. You must be out of your mind.'

Altieri's piggy eyes looked across the desk.

'No. Accessory to murder.'

The FBI man carefully watched Wallace's face, looking for the clues that reaction to such a statement might bring. He was disappointed. There was disbelief and amazement, but no guilt and no shock. Some anger, but he put that down to the assumption by the ex-CIA man that the inquiry might somehow be linked to the affair that had ended his career. Wallace looked across his desk at Altieri.

'You don't expect me to believe that do you?'

Altieri shrugged. 'I guess not; but it might make you realize that this is an official inquiry and the subject is murder.'

'Tell me.'

Altieri pointed to the trigger shoe still lying on Wallace's desk. 'We believe that that came off the murder gun, and that you supplied this actual shoe.'

'What makes you think that?'

Altieri pulled a notebook from his pocket and checked slowly through the pages. Then reading from his notes he said, 'You ordered a dozen trigger shoes from Henshaw's about six weeks ago. Yes?'

'Yes.'

Altieri nodded towards the desk. 'That was one of the shoes dispatched to you.'

'But they make thousands of them. All look-alike, exactly the same.'

The FBI man shook his head. 'Not this time. An apprentice hand-made twenty shoes. You got twelve of them, a private individual got one and they've still got the other seven. Well they did have. We've got them now. The private individual didn't like the shoe they sent him; said it was badly made and the checkering was rough so he returned it to them. They checked it and agreed with him. The apprentice had hand-filed the checkering and left the metal ridges coarse and unfinished. They put the shoes he had made on one side. They were going to write to you and suggest you send the duds back to them for standard replacements but they never got round to it. There are nine of them in your cardboard box. They're brighter than the others. That means there's three to account for.'

'And who got murdered?'

'A guy in Chicago. A builder. One single shot. Plumb on target.'

'Any idea of the weapon?'

'A 38 Walther PPK, as near as forensic can tell.'

'Any other clues?'

'Maybe.'

'How can I help?'

'Check through all your invoices for the last six weeks. See if you can trace any sales of trigger shoes.'

'They're a small-value sale, and they'd most likely be for cash.'

'OK. But check.'

'I'll get the invoices.'

As he walked behind the glass-topped counter and reached down for the box-file that held the invoices he knew exactly who had had the three trigger shoes. Matt Parsons at the club; old Percy out at Gannister's Farm, who was giving it to some nephew who was staying with them for a week. And the girl. Without even thinking about it he knew he wasn't going to mention her.

He carried the file back into the office, opened the lid, took out roughly half the invoices and handed them to Altieri.

'You do those. I'll do the rest.'

Both the invoiced trigger shoes were in Wallace's pile. He put them out, read them and then passed them to the FBI man.

Altieri finally re-checked all the invoices but nothing further was found.

'You don't remember a third one?'

'I'm afraid I don't.'

'I'll go out and see these two, but I don't think they'll be any use.'

'Why are you so sure?'

'It was a woman who did the killing.'

'How d'you know that?'

Altieri sighed professionally, bored with the vagaries of human stupidity. 'They found the trigger shoe in the room. A man wouldn't need a shoe on a PPK. And it seems the victim had been after a woman who was visiting the area looking for a house.'

'Have you got a description of her?'

'Dozens. But she left the motel where she was staying, the night of the murder. She checked in her rental car at O'Hare and that's the end of the trail. Nobody's flown out since then in her name.'

'What was her name and description?'

Altieri leafed back through his notes. 'Registered in the name of Anna Duchamps. Speaks good English but slight foreign accent. Aged about 25. Five nine or ten. Dark hair, brown eyes, good looking, appearance of being wealthy. And according to male witnesses, she's got nice tits and long legs.' Smiling, he closed his notebook. 'And I guess that's all we'll ever know about the lady.'

'What was the motive?'

Altieri shrugged. 'Public opinion in the area says he was probably trying to screw her and she wasn't having any, but that doesn't fit in. All descriptions indicate she was a very calm, cool chick who could have handled him without any trouble. He screwed around with a lot of young girls and there was no indication of any rough stuff. They were all willing volunteers. You haven't had anyone in the store answering to that description?'

Wallace shook his head. 'Not that I can recall. If I do I'll contact you.'

'Fine. I'm at the Dallas office. I'll just check those two customers out before I head back.'

'What was the name of the murdered man?'

'Jansen. Ludwig Jansen. Originally German, became a citizen just over twenty years ago.'

Wallace phoned Manton at the CIA's Chicago office that night. He was not available, but would be in the office on the Friday.

It had been Manton who had given Wallace and Wiczkowski the orders for the operation that eventually caused them to be dismissed. Manton's posting to Chicago had been part of the hair-shirt principle that tends to follow unsuccessful operations, particularly when they are in the public eye.

Manton met him when he landed at O'Hare; and they strolled over to the bar. After a couple of drinks Manton said, 'What is it you want, Hank?'

'I want to see every passenger list for flights from Chicago on the night of 7 September. And maybe the two following days.'

'Domestic or foreign?'

'Both.'

'What's it all about?'

'A girl.'

Manton smiled. 'Love or lust?'

'A bit of both, I guess.'

'It'll take a day to get them. They'll be on fiche or on film. You'll have to inspect them at our offices. You can make notes but not copies. OK?'

'OK.'

'Are you booked in anywhere?'

'Not yet.'

'I'll go and see the Airport Authority now, and then we'll get you fixed up.'

Wallace sat in front of the micro-film reader cursing his luck that O'Hare was the busiest airport in the whole United States, maybe the world. But at least it meant that it was probably the most efficient.

He scanned the individual flight lists for the night of September 7 from eight o'clock onwards. He was lighting a cigarette when he noticed the footnote that stated that passenger details were categorized under various headings. Name, sex, destination in seven categories, starting point of journey, fare paid and method of payment. These details were on a day by day basis.

He sorted through the reels and found the category files for three days. He checked the female listings first, and two hours later he had two possible names – Paulette Prouvost, passenger on a TWA flight to Miami, and Anna Simon, a passenger on an Air Canada flight to Toronto. He checked the starting point of journey for both passengers. For Paulette Prouvost the starting point had been Salt Lake City. She was 18, and her fare had been paid two months in advance through a student travel agency. Anna Simon was 27, her starting point was Chicago, and she paid cash for her ticket.

He phoned his father in Wichita Falls, and asked him to go over and look after the store with young Tom. He said that he might be away for a couple of weeks.

Manton checked for him with METRO police in Toronto.

They came back in a couple of hours. The girl had booked in at the Sutton Place Hotel for three nights and had flown to Amsterdam via Shannon. The home address she had given for the hotel register had been a non-existent street in Paris. But she had used an American Express card to pay for her Amsterdam flight and they gave Manton its serial number. By late evening he had the address, Villa des Fleurs, Aix-en-Provence, France.

Chapter Twelve

She lay on the bed, her eyes open, staring at the ceiling but not seeing it, her mind in a turmoil. Almost two weeks had gone by and she still had no plan as to how she could kill Stein. She had come to realize that she had had no plan as to how she would kill Jansen. Learning how to shoot and how to defend herself had seemed enough. And in the case of Jansen it *had* been enough. It had seemed so easy. Jansen was the kind of man she had visualized, typical of her vague picture of an SS man. Big, arrogant, self-confident. A male chauvinist pig before anybody had even thought of the description. She realized now that she had given no thought to what these men were like. They were just names in a letter without features, shape, lives or personalities. Perhaps if Jansen's killing had been more difficult she would have learned something. But it was too late now. She had to learn on Stein and she was making no progress.

On most days she had visited the gallery, alone or on a few occasions with Jan. She was always made welcome but there was always a continuous flow of visitors and friends. The few times when she had been invited up to the apartment above the gallery there were always one or two of Stein's blond young men who seemed to have the run of the place. Stein himself was always charming and hospitable but he made no move to be alone with her.

The first Sunday she had been in Amsterdam Stein had driven her out to his farm. There had been two or three boys there. Younger boys, who made their relationship with Stein even more obvious than the young men in Amsterdam. The farm manager's wife had provided a simple meal for them all, but the boys had only left when she and Stein left to drive back to Amsterdam.

It was on that journey that she decided that that would have been an opportunity to kill him if only she had planned in advance. But there seemed too many loose ends that her thinking wouldn't tie up. Dare she kill him as he was driving? What would happen to the car? What were the chances of an empty road? Somebody might see. Another car driver. How would she get back to Amsterdam? How could she be sure of getting out of Holland quickly? Amsterdam was too closed in, everybody was on top of everybody else. Stein wasn't the slightest bit interested in her as a woman. She could be here for months and still no further forward. And what turned her confusion into lethargy was the realization that even if she had spent more time in finding out the backgrounds of the four men it still wouldn't have helped her plan how to kill them. She knew plenty about Stein but it still didn't help her.

Despite the lethargy she had already bought an open air-ticket to Paris, and another to London. The part that seemed to defeat her was the impossibility of being alone with Stein in Amsterdam with a chance to get away. And doing it outside Amsterdam provided even more problems. The phone ringing startled her and she reached for it with her hand trembling.

'Hans Stein, is that Anna?'

'Yes, speaking.'

'You sound a bit down. Is anything the matter?'

'No. I was asleep when the phone rang.'

'How stupid of me. Forgive me. Look. I'm going to the farm tomorrow, would you like to come?'

'Of course. What time?'

'Could you come to the gallery about two. We'll be back in Amsterdam mid-evening, say eight o'clock. Does that suit you?'

'That would be fine.'

As she hung up she wondered if this could be her chance. On a week-day the boys would probably not be at the farm. She prepared herself for a hurried departure and wondered if there were other things she should do. If there were she couldn't think what they could be.

It was a beautiful sunny day as she walked to the gallery and she realized that it was the first time that she had really looked at the people and the streets. And sub-consciously she knew why. She didn't want to belong for a moment to the places where these men lived. She didn't want anything that would make her remember.

Stein was waiting for her, smiling and amiable as he locked the gallery. He drove the Mercedes roadster with care and skill, his gloved hands light on the wheel, his eyes glancing from time to time at the instruments. They were at the farm in half an hour. She had walked with him to the farm manager's cottage and he had talked for twenty minutes about the benefits of mixing their own pig feed and the savings they might make from buying and selling through the local farmers' co-operative. Eventually Stein stood up, looking at her.

'Let me take you across and show you the pig unit. I'm quite proud of it. Even though it does have to be subsidized by the gallery.' He laughed. 'Maybe it's a good sign when works of art make more money than producing pork and bacon.'

He left her standing in the yard for a few moments to go in the main farmhouse building. He came out with a bottle of red wine in one hand and two glasses in the other. Even in a farmyard Hans Stein managed to look quite sophisticated.

The pig unit was a long, broad, wooden building, obviously quite new, and inside was a small area where food bags were piled in a three sided square. She had walked with Stein down the long concrete gangway past farrowing pens and rearing pens. Large fans kept the temperature down and the grunting of the sows and the squeals of their litters seemed to be contented.

She leaned on the metal sty rails as Stein explained knowledgeably how it all worked. Showing her the weight charts and feeding records that hung at each pen. He turned and smiled at her.

'You must be utterly bored, my dear, with all this. Let's try that Mouton Cadet.'

They walked back to the food store and he closed the door to the rearing unit. He fished in his pocket, brought out a corkscrew and uncorked the bottle.

'It's a sin to drink it like this.'

He put it on the small desk and laid out two bags of feed for each of them to sit on.

When he had poured them each a full glass he sat down.

'Prosit,' he said, as he lifted his glass.

'Prosit,' she replied, and hated it.

'How much longer are you staying in our fair city, my dear?'

'I'm not sure, Hans. Maybe another week.'

'Have you seen what you want to see?'

'Most of it.'

'And have you done your business?'

'Most of it.'

'Tell me, what are things like in Berlin these days?'

She shrugged. 'All the usual problems, Hans. Nothing special.'

'The Kurfürstendamm?'

'Much the same.'

He leaned forward and topped up her glass as she put it down. Then, as he filled his own glass, he spoke without looking up at her.

'So tell me who you are, and why you're here.'

He leaned back, looking intently at her face. She felt suddenly cold, and, frowning, she put down her drink.

'I don't understand, Hans.'

'What don't you understand, Anna?'

'Your question.'

'Who are you, Anna? What's your real name?'

He put down his glass and leaned forward so that his face was close to hers.

'I told you already. My name is Anna Hartman.'

His hand grabbed her wrist, knocking over his glass as he reached across between them. She tried to stand but his strong hand bent back her wrist and then her arm until she cried out in pain.

'Who are you, woman?'

He stood up and kicked the desk to one side, the glasses and the bottle crashing to the floor, and the pain went like fire up to her shoulder so that to ease it she stood too. Then she screamed as his hand gripped one of her breasts, not with lust but anger. She could see his face in front of hers, twisted in anger like a mediaeval gargoyle.

'Where's your passport?'

'Let me go,' she moaned. 'I'll show it to you.'

As he released her arm she leaned back trembling against the stacks of pig feed. She put her hand to her head as she bent down to pick up her handbag. Her hands were shaking as she opened it slowly and took out her passport. He snatched it from her hand and saw at once that it was a French passport. His eyes went quickly over each page as he turned them.

And as he looked her hand closed round the gun. It made only a slight clink as the barrel touched the gilt frame of her handbag, but he heard it and his head came up. She saw the surprise as his eyes lifted from the gun to her face.

'You wouldn't be so . . .'

The first shot was low. It took him in the stomach, knocking him backwards against the other pile of feed bags and then, with the pistol almost touching his chest she fired again. He groaned, and then, with one hand pressed to his chest his body slid down and sideways. She saw blood spattered on the brown paper of the feed bags, and a stream of dry pellets poured from a rent in one of the bags. For a moment she stood paralysed, watching the stream of food forming a pyramid on Stein's torso.

Then, as if she were suddenly alive again, she thrust the pistol back in her handbag, picked up her passport from the floor and made for the door. At the door she stopped, turned, and walked back to where Stein's body lay. She hadn't the courage to put her hand inside his shirt to feel for his heart but as her fingers felt for a pulse in his wrist she could feel the coldness of his flesh. There was no sign of life. She stood up and walked back to the door.

Outside she closed her eyes for a moment against the bright sunlight, then as she half opened them she could see the glitter of the sun on the car's chrome where it stood outside the manager's cottage. It was four hundred metres away but instinct told her not to touch it. She turned and walked back down the length of the pig unit and across a meadow thick with daisies and buttercups. She skirted a windbreak of young poplars and made for the road. Despite her raised arm the private cars ignored her, but a truck ground to a halt alongside her. The driver spoke only Dutch but he nodded to her to get in.

As the truck slowly picked up speed she offered the driver two ten guilder notes. He grinned, took one of them and pushed the other aside. He nodded when she said Amsterdam. On the inside of the cab were pictures cut from magazines, footballers, cyclists and naked girls. The road seemed a long way below them as she looked down on the top of the cars that passed them in the fast lane.

A few kilometres later he spoke in Dutch, briefly turning to look at her, smiling. It sounded like a question. She smiled and shrugged to show that she didn't understand. He reached out, took her hand and put it on the bulge at his crotch. The movement of his body indicated in any language what he wanted her to do. For a brief moment she wondered whether he would be able to give a better description of her to the police if she did it or didn't do it. And there was always the possibility that he would stop the truck and make her get out if she didn't comply. Slowly her hand moved on him as he drove until eventually she felt him climax. He turned to look at her, smiling, his lips pouting a kiss.

He had dropped her by the Central Station and she had

hurried to her hotel. As she looked at her watch she saw it was almost exactly an hour since she had fled from the farm.

She had hurriedly washed and changed, packed her bag, paid her bill and taken a taxi the short distance back to the station.

It was ten o'clock when she arrived in The Hague, and just after midnight she was undressing in her cabin on the night boat from the Hook to Harwich. For the first time in ten days she slept soundly.

There was a security check at Harwich. Her case was searched thoroughly and a woman security officer ran the electronic detector over her body. The typewriter was opened, checked briefly and then passed to the clearing bench.

She stayed in London for two days and booked a flight to Marseilles from Gatwick. In the second morning's *Daily Express* and *The Times* there was a brief paragraph reporting the unexplained killing of a well-known Amsterdam art-dealer. The Dutch police were investigating but no further details were given. Not even Stein's name.

The lethargy had gone. Lost as she slept on the Channel crossing. On the train from Amsterdam to the Hague she had wondered if the farmer or his wife had heard the shots and had wondered if Jan might be involved in the investigation. They would put two and two together but there was no way they could check her real identity. The second passport in the name of Duchamps had cost her 5,000 New Francs in Marseilles, and even if the immigration officer's checking had not been so cursory it would have stood up to everything short of a full forensic examination. The only mistake she had made was in forgetting to pick up the two ejected shell-cases at the farm. She knew that for a couple of minutes she had panicked. Her mind had never envisaged a challenge. Resistance, maybe, but not a pre-emptive attack. But having survived she was now better prepared. Nobody would surprise her again. It was like passing an examination, a driving test. She had passed. Jansen and Stein were strangers again. No longer a part of her life.

She looked at the Thames, the Houses of Parliament, and Buckingham Palace, with recognition but indifference. Just once her calm was broken. She hired a radio from a nearby shop because the hotel radio only gave her the BBC programmes, and she needed to hear something French. She was listening to *France Inter*, a record request programme, as she brushed her hair, and without thinking she hummed along as they played an old Charles Trenet song. Suddenly she recognized the words. Paul had sung it almost every day while he was washing and shaving. For several seconds she stood there, frozen, listening. '... *biens des gens s'arrêtent, et la voix émue, cent façons répètent la vielle chanson des rues* ...' And then she had struck at the front of the radio with the handle of the brush, again and again, the glass tuning scale shattering, the plastic case cracking. Then, a flash and a smell of burning as she stood there, trembling, her chest heaving as she searched blindly for the bed and sat down and wept. So many times he had sung it, off-key, stumbling over the words, and smiling as he looked at her face. With her hands over her face she sobbed as if she would never stop. She wanted to fling herself on the bed but instead she stumbled to the bathroom and filled the bowl with cold water. The cold water lapped at her ears as she plunged her face deep in the bowl. Then bringing up her face she dried it with a towel without looking in the mirror. Automatically she reached for her handbag, and slamming the bedroom door behind her she took the elevator down to the restaurant. She had pulled down the shutters of her mind before she had finished the meal.

She had taken no risk and swallowed just one of the pale blue capsules with her wine. She was pleasantly, soothingly sleepy as she undressed.

Chapter Thirteen

She phoned the villa from the airport at Marseilles. Pierre was in Aix, but Jean-Louis would come and pick her up in the Fiat.

She found that she could no longer sit calmly. Her self-control seemed to have gone and she paced nervously around the almost empty foyer, waiting impatiently. Twice she went to the ladies room to wash her hands and face, and apply new lipstick. At the bookstall she found the sales-woman's eyes on her and she realized that she was tidying the piles of magazines at the front of the stall. She bought a copy of that morning's *Figaro* and sat at a table in the res-taurant with a whisky and a coffee. She looked at the front page of the newspaper but her mind wouldn't absorb the words. She felt very near to tears.

It was almost an hour and a half later that she looked up and saw her father-in-law's big figure pushing aside the swing door and walking towards her. She stood up, reaching for her typewriter and handbag.

'Anna.'

'*Beau-père.*'

And then his arms were around her and he was kissing her forehead.

'We are a little late because Jean-Louis knew that I should want to be here and it took time for him to track me down in Aix.'

He held her away from him, looking at her face, his head to one side.

'Younger, she looks, but too thin. We'll soon put that right. Give me your case.'

'My luggage is in the hall.'

'Jean-Louis can bring that. He's lurking impatiently over there, impatient to see our young lady again.'

Jean-Louis had already found her cases and had loaded them into the car. And now he stood beaming as they walked towards him.

'Here she is, Jean-Louis, back in the fold again. Back home.'

Jean-Louis had given his little bow and the three of them had walked to the car.

Outside she breathed deeply, and despite the fumes of oil and petrol she could smell again that unmistakable smell of Provence. A hot greenhouse smell, a mixture of rich earth and mimosa, lush foliage and ozone.

As they swept on to the road to Aix she saw the hills again. She was leaning forward to look out of the window and as her eyes took in the blue skies and the wooded hills she suddenly felt at home again. She sighed, leaned back, and closed her eyes.

She was still asleep when they drew up at the villa. And Pierre Simon sat unmoving with his arm round her, her head on his shoulder.

'Leave the cases, Jean-Louis. The sleep will do her good.'

It was almost two hours later when she stirred and slowly woke. He saw the caution in her eyes as she looked around her, it was like an animal waking and checking out its territory. Then, sighing, she turned to look at him.

'It's so nice to be back.'

For a week she walked through the woods and across the hills, taking a hamper with her, lying in the sun, sleeping and reading.

Pierre asked her no questions about where she had been. And at dinner at night he talked of the latest exhibitions in the Paris galleries, new novels and the latest offering of the Comédie Française. There was nothing personal. They never talked of his life, or Paul or herself. She knew that it was deliberate and sensed that for some reason it was for her sake, not his.

It was on the evening of her tenth day back that she broke the taboo. Deliberately.

'Do you think you might ever marry again, *beau-père?*'

He smiled and shook his head. 'No. I'm quite sure I shall not.'

'Why not?'

He steepled his big hands and touched them to his forehead as if it were some ritual. Then he looked up at her, putting his hands on the table.

'If it had been a nice quiet rustic marriage, and I were not so old, then perhaps I might consider a second marriage. But we shared too much horror, too much . . .' he searched for the word '. . . too much filth. She was much more than a wife. We weren't really a couple after the war. We were just one person. The baby made a big difference. Both great joy and great fear.'

'Why fear, Pierre?'

He sighed and shifted a glass before he spoke. His voice was low when he spoke and he didn't look up.

'Fear that those things could happen to him.'

She lit a cigarette and he looked at her face.

'I didn't know you smoked.'

'I do now, Pierre. And sometimes I drink a whisky.'

'What did you like about Paul?'

'It's hard to say. I just liked everything about him. He was handsome but he didn't seem to know it. He was gentle, wise, generous minded, and he listened to what people said. Even me.'

'I think you should think some day of marrying again. In good time.'

'Why?'

'I always felt you were a good partner for Paul. You would be a good partner for a similar man.'

She shook her head and her breath caught as she spoke.

'I regret many things I said to him, *beau-père.*'

'Tell me.'

She closed her eyes. 'I can remember once saying to him that he lived in an ivory tower and should find out what the world is really like.'

'What did he say?'

'Nothing. He just smiled. He must have despised me for my stupidity.'

'He was more likely pleased that his cover was that good.'

'I wish I could see him just once and take it all back.'

'That's what people always forget.'

'What?'

'That when they say good-bye in the morning that could be the last time they will ever see each other.'

'Does your religion help you? Does it comfort you now?'

He shook his head. 'I wish it did. In a way it is a comfort, like the home you were born in. To be a Jew is important to me, the religion not. Do you find comfort anywhere, my love?'

'I don't want comfort, Pierre. But I can cope now. I can bear it.'

They had had a last drink and then she had gone to her room.

As always she looked at the photograph before she went to sleep.

Chapter Fourteen

The man and the two girls looked at the wet Cibachrome print as it lay on the darkroom table. The man was wearing a blue-denim shirt and denim slacks. A paisley scarf was knotted neatly at his throat. The girls were naked. Giggling as they looked at the picture.

'Those longer eyelashes are much better, Wally.'

He laughed. 'They won't be looking at your eyelashes, sweetheart.'

'How do you get that sort of misty effect?'

'I put a filter over the lens with a film of vaseline at the edges.'

'How much do they pay you for them?'

He stood up, hands on hips, a rather elegant man.

'That's none of your business, sweetie.'

'D'you get more for these shots than the porn stuff?'

'About the same. Now, beat it, and I'll get your cash.'

As they walked into the studio he called over his shoulder:

'Judy. I want a word with you.'

He put the print in the drying rack and switched on the heater. Then he turned to look at the girl.

'D'you want to stay tonight, kid?'

'If you want, Wally. It's up to you.'

He leaned back with his hands on the edge of the sink.

'How much d'you want?'

'Same as usual. Fifty for the night.'

'You get a lot of studio work from me, you know.'

She grinned. 'Opening my legs for a Hasselblad isn't the same as opening them for you.'

He laughed softly. 'You're a cheeky little bitch. It's a good job you've got big tits.'

He smacked her behind and gave her two envelopes.

'Give Rosie hers and then go upstairs to my place when she's gone. I'll be another ten minutes down here.'

'D'you want me to get dressed?'

He looked at her thoughtfully. 'Yeah. It'll make a change.'

Walther Müller had a wife in Bolivia. He hadn't seen her for fifteen years. Like a good many top Nazi, he used the quite legitimate excuse that it was easier for the hunters to identify their victims if there was a family. And like most of the others he found it more congenial to live alone without responsibilities. She was paid regularly but parsimoniously by the ODESSA, and he had almost forgotten her existence.

He had come to England in 1960 with a genuine Irish passport that had cost a thousand US dollars; and a draft on the Bank of Bilbao for £27,000. For the first three years he had leased the shop and the flat above it but when the business was established and making good money he had bought the property and the leasehold.

After a few years he had a south London accent just short of Cockney. The name he used was Miller and so far as he could tell nobody knew that he, was originally German.

The shop and flat were not in the main shopping area. There was sense in not getting too big, not drawing attention to himself or prompting rivals to look for skeletons in the cupboard. But the profits were enough for him to have paid off by 1970 his financial obligations to the ODESSA. And once a year they got a payment from him that was gratefully received. Walther Müller was a much valued member of the ODESSA. A man who paid his dues.

He got on well with most people. Even in the old days he had been able to cover a cold ruthlessness with a jokey, artificial charm. His elegance and his coarse playboy good looks somehow made his Gestapo uniform less real. But there were SOE girls and men who had testified to the animal ferocity behind the hand-kissing. The documents that were the main evidence at his trial 'in absentia', in Paris, alleged that he was responsible for the death of 19 members of the Resistance. Four of them English, the others French. The documents alleged that two of the SOE girls had been burnt alive in Mauthausen concentration camp on Müller's personal orders. There was evidence that he had been directly responsible for the torture and death of 224 German citizens apart from thousands of Jews, and that evidence had been copied and transmitted to the German prosecutor at Düsseldorf.

In the vicinity of his shop and flat Wally Miller was a popular man in the clubs and pubs and the betting shops. The shop itself was well-stocked with cameras, lenses, dark-room equipment, with all the prices well discounted. On the first floor was the studio for portraits. There was no wedding photography but a fair turnover in mother and baby pictures. After the shop was closed each night the studio changed character. And on two nights a week Wally Miller gave instruction in glamour photography. There were generally eight or nine enthusiasts at these sessions and Miller's responsibilities did not go far beyond providing the lighting, the models, and suggesting that the best results could be obtained if the lens cap was actually removed. His introductions always included a set-piece about the importance of the model-photographer relationship. An appreciative but arms-length relationship was what Wally recommended. The essence of glamour, Wally would say, was not naked-ness but creativity.

On the other evenings the studio was devoted to more esoteric photography by the maestro himself, and some of the prettier, and perhaps greedier, young housewives and typists in the Croydon area would pose for photographs that a few weeks later would provide uplift for tired businessmen in Hamburg or Hanover. Despite the high model fees he made more out of each of these sessions than the shop made in a month. And there were perks of course. What show-biz discreetly refers to as 'management privileges'. And one of those perks was the girl Judy.

Judy was prettier than most film starlets, and the photographs of her lush young body were in constant demand from Hamburg to Cairo. She was ambitious but not promiscuous, and with her fees from Miller averaging £400 a week she considered her session in his bed as more a form of insurance than anything else. And there was nothing kinky about Miller's sex. It was protracted but quite straightforward.

He poured them both a whisky and as he sipped the warming liquid he looked over the top of his glass at the girl. She was breathtakingly pretty, and although he slept with a number of girls, she was the only one that he ever felt a need to impress. He wondered sometimes if it wouldn't be a good idea to marry her. But there could be snags and he had never pursued it.

'You'd better bring that other blonde wig tomorrow, Sweetie. The waved one.'

'It's here, Wally. In the prop cupboard.'

'And don't wear pants tomorrow, they leave marks on you.'

She smiled. 'So do you. D'you want to go upstairs now?'

'Yes. Let's do that.'

He was having her for the second time, slowly and skilfully, his hands fondling her full breasts, their mouths clamped avidly together, when the telephone rang, loudly and imperatively. But Müller was, as navigators say, beyond the point of no return. And the phone had rung continuously while he was bringing events to a satisfactory conclusion, which, in a way, was just as well, because it was the last time in his life that Müller was going to have a girl.

But we often cross our Rubicons without knowing it, and he had finally disentangled their bodies and reached for the phone.

'Wally Miller, who is it?'

The girl lay listening, surprised at his sudden anger, and even more surprised that he was talking in German, quite unresponsive to her wandering hand.

He had crashed the receiver back on to the cradle and turned to look at her.

'I'll have to take you home, Judy.'

'For Christ's sake, it's nearly three o'clock. I've told my parents I'm staying with a girl-friend.'

He closed his eyes for a moment, trying to think.

'OK, you stay here. I've got to go out and pick someone up. I shan't bring him in this room. If you see him at all don't talk to him. Don't answer any questions. Understood?'

'OK, Wally, keep it cool. Will you be coming back to bed?'

'I don't think so. I'll be dealing with this lunatic.'

He dressed hurriedly and picked up his car keys from the bedside table.

He circled the East Croydon roundabout twice before he saw Altman standing under the canopy at the entrance to the Fairfield Hall. He flashed his headlights and watched Altman walk over towards the car. He swore under his breath. The fool walked as if he were on parade in the Unter den Linden.

He leaned over and opened the door on the passenger side. Altman bent down, grinning as he looked at Müller's face.

'Heil Hitler,' he said, as he got in the car.

'Cut it out, you bloody fool.'

He drove in silence to the South Croydon junction, pulled in by the 'Swan' car-park, and switched off the ignition. He turned to look at Altman.

'What the hell are you doing here, Fritz?'

'They've sent me over, Walther. To put you in the picture. There's trouble and they want you to deal with it.'

'What trouble?'

'You know Jansen's dead?'

'Ludwig Jansen?'

'Yes.'

'What happened?'

'He was shot. Murdered. Hans Stein is dead too.'

'What happened to him?'

'He was shot as well.'

Müller looked at Altman. 'What the hell's going on?'

'We don't know exactly. But we want you to deal with it. They sent me over to tell you what we know and to give you instructions.'

'Instructions about what?'

'Dealing with the killer.'

'You mean the same man killed them both?'

'It wasn't a man, it was a woman.'

Müller's disbelief silenced him for a moment, and then he said, 'Who says it was a woman?'

'The FBI and the Netherlands police, both have a woman as their number one suspect. Both of them were shot with a .38 PPK. They reckon that both bullets were from the same gun.'

'When did this happen?'

'They both happened in the last four or five weeks.'

'Who is the woman?'

'That's what they want you to find out.'

'How bloody ridiculous. Why not let the police find her?'

Altman smiled. 'You mean after she's killed you and Trommer.'

'Why me? Why Trommer?'

'Because you and Trommer and Jansen and Stein were the four appointed to deal with the counter-moves against the Jews.'

Müller's mouth dropped open as he tried to absorb the information. Then he said slowly and almost in a whisper. 'Jesus Christ, where does it all end?'

114

'When you find the woman, Walther. If she doesn't find you first.'

Müller was silent for several minutes, his fingers on the ignition key. He turned to look at Altman.

'Have they got a description of her?'

'Yes. It won't help you much. There's a hundred thousand women who could answer to the description we've got.'

Müller started the engine. 'I'll take you back to my place. There's a girl there. Don't talk to her. Don't talk in front of her.'

He made up a bed for Altman from cushions on the settee in the living-room.

The girl was asleep when Müller went back in the bedroom, and the next morning he woke her early and took her for breakfast at a local hotel. She didn't ask him about the events of the previous evening or about the man she had seen sleeping on the settee. And he had dismissed it as a visit by an old friend who was down on his luck.

He opened the shop and manned it until the manager arrived and then went upstairs to arouse Altman.

When Altman had dressed and eaten, Müller started to question him.

'Give me the description of the woman.'

'Between twenty-five and thirty, about one metre seventy, dark hair, good figure, speaks English fluently but with a slight foreign accent. Goes under the name of Anna Duchamps. There's no confirmation or contradiction as to whether that is really her name.'

'How did you get the information?'

'From a newspaper crime reporter in Chicago and a policeman in Amsterdam. The United States police and the Netherlands police haven't connected the two murders yet. It's unlikely they ever will; and we don't propose to inform them.'

'Why not?'

'We daren't draw attention to ourselves. Even if we tipped

115

them off anonymously they would start putting two and two together. At the moment they have no idea what the motive was in either case. Because it's a woman it's taken for granted that it's a sex thing. An *affaire* of some kind.'

'How do they expect me to find her on this information?'

Altman shrugged. 'They've no idea. They're too far out of the picture. You've no idea how we live down there.'

'Don't give me that crap, Fritz. You were all sitting cushy while the rest of us were being hounded round Europe.'

Altman put his arm round Müller's shoulders as if to instil some sense of camaraderie into the situation, but Müller looked away impatiently, ignoring the gesture and Altman himself.

He was trying to list in his mind the areas or groups that the assassin could come from. And at the same time he was trying to think of how to get rid of Altman. It was like carrying a bomb to have him around. He turned to look at him, anxious to find some grounds for sending him on his way.

'How did you come in, Fritz?'

Altman smiled. 'The Monsignore's pilot flew me to Rio and then I got a commercial flight to London via Lisbon.'

'What passport have you got?'

'Bolivian.'

'Forged or genuine?'

'Genuine document but forged stamp.'

'When are you going back?'

'I'll stay and help if you want.'

'For God's sake, Fritz, you can barely speak the language. You'd stick out like a sore thumb.'

'I could do the rough stuff for you.'

Müller looked at Altman's face. It was a deep brown with the scars from old sores on his cheeks and forehead. And his eyes were like the eyes of a dog that got nothing but kicks but thought that perhaps its luck had changed. Despite his anger and impatience he felt a twinge of sympathy for the man.

'Thanks for the offer but no. I've got all that sort of help I need. You know that. But you can stay for a couple of days. Have you got money?'

Altman grinned. 'Plenty. Some of it's for you.'

'Keep it. I don't need it. Have a bath, relax, and this afternoon I'll take you shopping. Get you some clothes and shoes. Tonight I'll take you to dinner. We'll book you a return flight this afternoon for tomorrow evening.'

Altman nodded reluctantly and then he looked across at Müller. 'Any chance of a girl for tonight?'

For a moment Müller hesitated. Altman looked more like a jungle Indian than a European. His rough clothes, his jagged hair-cut and his tanned face. And he stank like an animal. An acrid smell that would perhaps go unnoticed in the jungle where he lived, but in a small room was overpowering and unpleasant. But he nodded.

'Yes. I'll find a girl for you.'

Altman grinned, rubbing his hands together and Müller could barely hide his disgust.

Müller waited with Altman until the passengers for Lisbon were called and then drove back to Croydon. The journey gave him time to think. In thirty-six hours he had eliminated most of the possible sources of an assassin. The ODESSA had contacts in Tel Aviv and Jerusalem, and it was clear that neither MOSSAD nor any of their special units had been involved. The contact who supplied information from the Jewish Documentation Centre in Vienna was always reliable in his assessments, but the security of the Centre was too personal and too great for much actual information to come out. But the source had said that there were no indications at all that the Centre had initiated an attack on the four ODESSA men. He was also quite sure that the Centre had no knowledge of the counter-attack that the four had been ordered to carry out.

The only motive left was personal revenge on the part of

117

someone connected with one of the two men who had been killed in the new ODESSA counter-attack. Müller felt sure that the woman wanted by the police was no more than a decoy or an accomplice. A lone woman was not going to tackle the men who had trampled their way over Europe.

Müller had read the brief notes. There had been two ODESSA revenge killings since the orders had gone out from the monastery in the Matto Grosso, and Müller read the brief notes that Altman had brought for him. The first victim had been a man in Düsseldorf named Moshe Raski. A German Jew who had worked in the Public Prosecutor's office. He had photocopied over three hundred files on senior Nazis in the past ten years. The copies had gone to the Documentation Centre in Vienna, to an address in Tel Aviv, and particular files had gone to certain Israeli embassies. Information had been passed to the media that led to organized pressure for individual prosecutions of nineteen men accused of complicity in major war-crimes against the Jews. Eight of the accused had been sentenced to long terms of imprisonment despite the ODESSA's hiring of top advocates to defend them. Using the procedures of the law in one country or another had enabled the other trials to be postponed again and again until the public and the prosecution were bored with the proceedings. Four men had been extradited to stand trial in Jerusalem, and one of them had already been sentenced to death. According to the notes, Raski had been in Belsen-Bergen for four years and his wife had died in Ravensbrück in 1943. It was believed that he had a brother who had emigrated to Australia. There were no other close associates or relatives known to the ODESSA. Raski had been shot at point-blank range while looking at a menu in the window of a restaurant on the Königsallee. Nobody, apart from Raski, had been killed or injured. An amount to cover the replacement of the broken window had been sent anonymously to the owner of the restaurant. The ODESSA had telephoned the media in the name of the Baader-Meinhof gang, claiming that the killing was theirs. The ODESSA man who had carried out the instructions had returned quietly to Portugal the same night.

The second killing interested Müller more. According to the record, Paul Simon had a wife. The record listed her as being German, and in her late twenties. The man who had been killed on the street by the falling masonry was Jean Paul Didier and he too had a wife. He also had a mistress. There was a cutting from *Le Figaro* that gave details of the hospital where Madame Simon had been taken. He would start his inquiries there, but he saw it as unlikely that a German girl would tackle the ODESSA. Apart from that there was no way she could have dreamed up a connection between her husband's death and the ODESSA. And there was certainly no way she could have found out about the committee of four. In the end it would turn out to be some Israeli bitch from one of their special squads.

Müller spent the afternoon booking himself on to a flight to Paris from Gatwick and handing over the shop to his manager.

Müller's French was poor, and he waited around in his hotel until Boudon came in from Lyons. Boudon had been a member of the Milice, the Frenchmen who helped the Gestapo and the SD do their dirty work during the occupation. When Müller had phoned him he'd been non-committal until the German had indicated a fee of a thousand New Francs plus expenses.

The receptionist sent them to the almoner's office who had been hesitant about giving any details about a patient. But when Boudon said that he needed the girl's address so that an insurance claim could be paid to the wife of the passer-by who had been killed, she gave him Pierre Simon's Paris address.

The concièrge at the apartment block had told them that Monsieur Simon was at his villa in Aix. And that had been enough. She was not able to give the address, but the Central Post Office had the appropriate telephone directory. It gave the name of the villa but nothing more, apart from the telephone number.

They had a meal together and then Müller checked out of his hotel and went to the station.

Chapter Fifteen

Wallace drove the hire-car slowly past the open gate of the villa. All he could see was the stone wall that curved round the patio, and the steps leading upwards until they were hidden in a gush of bougainvillaea. The hill road wound up and up and then turned south again, away from the villa and the estate. He found a small path into the woods and parked the car in the shadow of the beeches. He reached over to the back seat and grabbed the leather strap of the binoculars.

When he estimated that he was a mile inside the woods he turned westwards. Ten minutes later he was at the edge of the woods. The villa was further away than he expected, but as he used the glasses he could see the patio at the side and the front of the villa. There were two coloured umbrellas and white garden tables and chairs, but no sign of people. He looked at his watch. It was four-thirty.

He lay the glasses down beside him and lit a cigarette, cupping the flame in his hands. It was over an hour later when he saw her. Not where he expected, at the villa, but walking slowly up the hill towards the villa on the far side of the valley. He realized that she must have come from the hillside where he sat. From further along the edge of the wood. Hidden, perhaps, by dead ground until she reached the far side.

He focused the glasses carefully. It was the girl all right. He couldn't see her face, but the way she walked and the long black hair were enough. Then she turned, and shading her eyes with her hand, she looked back towards the woods before carrying on up the slope to the villa gardens. Slowly he brought down the glasses and rested them on his knees. It seemed odd to see her in her own environment. When he was tracking her down it had seemed a sensible thing to do.

But, in fact, he had never actually visualized what he would do or say when they met. The fact that it was almost certain that she had killed a man, he had brushed aside. His own training, and his training of others, was never concerned with moral issues. What the 'target' had done, or might do, was only of concern if it helped the surveillance or the hunt. And what were his motives? To expose her? To watch her? To find out what was behind it? He knew all too well that it was none of those reasons. He cared about her, missed her, wanted her. And the killing in Chicago gave him a reason, an excuse, to do what he wanted to do anyway.

He saw her go through the blue door in the garden wall, and even when he could no longer see her, he felt a kind of excitement. An excitement tinged with doubt or foreboding. He wasn't sure which. His feelings were rather like those long months when he was at high school and head over heels in love with a pretty girl whose father owned half the properties on the main drag. It had lasted a whole summer of walking and talking. Hands had been held, and there had been two or three gentle kisses, but nothing more. The affection would almost certainly have grown into love, or at least a falling in love; but it had had no chance to grow. A short note from the girl's father to his mother had ended it before the autumn term had started. It had been polite, definite and brutal. He barely remembered the details now, but he could remember the girl and the summer, and the vague feeling of apprehension that had lurked at the edge of those summer days. He had that same feeling now. A feeling that it would be wise to get in the car and head for the airport and Stanton Falls.

He wound the leather strap of the binoculars round his hand and stood up. There was just a faint taste of autumn in the air, and in the wood it was chilly and beginning to lose its colours in the dusk. He drove slowly back to Aix. But he knew now what he would do.

From nine o'clock to mid-day there had been no movement

122

from the house. The windows to the patio were open but the only movement was a magazine or a newspaper on one of the white circular garden tables ruffled by the breeze. But now that the breeze had fallen, even that slight movement had stopped.

He ate his cheese and fruit, poured himself coffee from the Thermos and settled down to wait out the afternoon. It was only a few minutes later that he saw the man come out on to the patio. Wallace lifted the glasses. The man was big but his movements were slow and easy; in one hand he carried a book and in the other a long glass. He turned to speak to someone in the shadow of the inner room, nodded, and then settled himself comfortably in one of the garden chairs.

Then he saw her. She was wearing a white blouse and a white pleated skirt, short socks and a pair of white sneakers. She walked over to the man, bent, and kissed his head.

It was five minutes before she came through the blue door in the garden wall. She closed it carefully behind her and stood in the hot afternoon sun looking across the valley. He watched her follow a path down the side of the hill, then cross a wooden bridge at the end of a lake. She stood on the near bank of the stream, looking down at the water, then crouching, she put her hand in the water letting it drift with the current. He saw her straighten up and move along the bank to where a line of spaced stones forded the stream. Then she was walking up the hill towards the edge of the wood about a quarter of a mile from where he was sitting. She was hidden now, in the dead ground from a spur of the hill.

He stood and gathered up his belongings into the canvas bag, keeping the binoculars hanging round his neck. There was a bridle path through the woods but no signs that it had been recently ridden. It was mainly a thick layer of dried leaves from decades of autumns and there was almost no noise from his footsteps. Just under a quarter of a mile a pathway cut across and led down towards the slope of the hillside. He hesitated for a moment and then took the pathway where it turned to the left. There was a dampness in the air and there were clusters of bright fungi on the back of the trees and scattered where their root structures gripped the earth. It was a few minutes later that he heard the sound of water and he saw the stream where it slid over an outcrop of rock to fall twenty or thirty feet to a pool that foamed white where the cascade of water met its surface. And on a flat rock sat the girl, leaning back against the bole of a willow tree, her hand dangling idly in the pool.

Although she was probably no further than fifty yards from where he stood it had taken him almost fifteen minutes to find a way down to her. He stood barely ten feet away from her but she had not heard him coming because of the noise of the waterfall.

He called out. 'Hi,' and she looked the wrong way because his voice echoed off the semi-circle of rocks. And then she saw him. She didn't recognize him and when he walked towards her he stopped a few feet away.

'Hello, Anna. It's only me, Hank Wallace.'

He could see her trying to sort out the data. It's not easy to recognize people you know quite well when you see them out of their normal setting. Then he saw the recognition flood her face. Not with pleasure, not even neutrality, but confusion and resentment. She wound herself up and stood there hands on hips.

'What on earth are you doing here, Hank?'

'And I'm pleased to see you too.'

But she ignored the plea and the irony.

'You haven't answered me.'

He smiled. 'I've brought you some coffee. Thought you might be thirsty.'

She pushed a long hank of her dark hair back over her shoulder, squinting against a ray of sunlight through the trees as she stared at him. She saw the disappointment on his face.

'Shall I go, Anna?'

She shivered despite the heat. 'No. Of course not. Let's walk out to the sunshine.'

He stood awkwardly to let her pass and lead the way. As she passed him she stopped and turned round to look at him.

'I'm sorry, Hank. It was a shock.'

'That's OK, honey, let's find that sun.'

At the edge of the wood she sat down and patted the grass beside her. As he settled himself he deliberately looked away from her across the valley.

'And how are you, girl?'

'Much the same. How are you? And Tom?'

'He's fine. Looking after the store with his grandad while the old man makes the grand tour of Europe.'

The clear hazel eyes looked at his face and she said softly, 'You're not the kind to do the grand tour, Hank. Why did you come?'

'To see you.'

'No other reason?'

'Not really.'

She leaned forward, snapped off a long blade of couch grass and put it between her teeth. Still looking at him she said, 'How did you find where I was?'

'Cashed in some old credits.'

'But why?'

'Like I said. I wanted to see you again. Thought maybe I could help some way.'

'Help with what?'

'Anything.'

She was silent for a few moments. 'Where are you staying?'

'At a pension in Aix. Pension Marignane.'

'How long have you been in Aix?'

'Today's the second day.'

'When are you leaving?'

His pale blue eyes looked at her face to see her reaction.

125

'When I've helped you.'

She knew then that he knew something. She felt cold and there was goose-flesh on her arms. But how could he know? If he knew anything then the police would know as much, and there would have been some attempt to question her. Perhaps he was bluffing. But she knew that he wasn't that kind of man.

She felt his warm, dry hand on her wrist, and she turned her head to look at him. The pale blue eyes looked at her face as he spoke.

'Nobody except me knows *who* you are, or *where* you are. You're under no obligation to me. Nobody knows that I've ever met you, and I shall never tell them.'

She sat in silence, chewing the blade of grass. Then she said, 'Will you answer me one question absolutely truthfully?'

'I'll answer all your questions truthfully.'

'I mean with no holding back. The whole truth.'

'OK.'

'You could have stayed in Texas and still not told anybody what you thought you knew. Why did you come here?'

It seemed a long time before he answered, and then he said quietly. 'Because I like you. Because I care about you. I wanted to help you.'

'Another lame duck?'

'By no means. You don't need to be a lame duck to need help. We all need help sometime or other.'

'When did you last need help?'

He looked at her face. 'I need help right now.'

'From me?'

'Yes.'

'Why do you need help?'

'Because I love you, and I don't know what to do about it.'

She recognized the same flat sadness in his voice that she had had in her own voice when she first came down to the villa from the hospital and Pierre had made her talk.

'You don't really know anything about me, Hank.'

He noticed the change, the softness, in her voice. He half-smiled. 'When I really know you then I shall be able to like you as well.'

'How do you know I'm not married?'

'I asked about the villa at the pension. They said it was owned by a very wealthy man named Simon and that his daughter-in-law lived there. There had been a tragedy.'

'What else did they say?'

'Nothing else. I didn't ask more.'

'I'll have to go, Hank, or my father-in-law will be worried.'

'Does he know about . . . about anything?'

She shook her head. 'Nothing at all. And he mustn't know.'

'Can I walk you back to the blue door?'

She raised here eyebrows. 'I seem to be under surveillance.' Then she held out her hand. 'Help me up.'

When he pulled her up she was close to him. She stood looking up at his tanned face. 'Will you meet me here tomorrow, Hank? By the waterfall.'

'Of course. What time?'

'Is eleven too early?'

He laughed softly. 'Of course not. I'll be here, waiting for you.'

She reached out for his hand as they stumbled down the hill on the rough pathway.

At the blue door she kissed him and without looking back went through to the garden.

He walked back slowly and it was almost an hour before he saw his car. Just before he got to the car he passed a man pushing a bicycle up the path into the woods. They nodded to each other and passed without speaking.

Some instinct made Wallace go early to meet the girl, and after parking his car at the entrance to the woods, he walked up the bridle-path. He had gone about two hundred yards

127

when he saw the glint of metal in the morning sun. He walked over to the clump of gorse and pulled the prickly branches apart. The reflection was from a bell on the handlebars of an old-fashioned bicycle.

He looked around but there was no one in sight. He walked slowly and quietly, deeper into the woods, towards the point where the plateau gave way to the hill down to the valley. At the edge of the wood he stood still and waited, scanning the hillside and the far slope of the hill up to the villa. Everywhere was silent except for the cooing of wood-pigeons and the distant drone of a plane. There was a slight mist rising from the ground from the heat of the early morning sun, and a brightly coloured cock-pheasant stood with one leg raised, its head to one side, listening before he walked into the sunshine. It was then he heard the chink of metal on metal, forward and over to his right. He took two careful steps forward and then he could see him. He was wearing a dark green shirt and brown trousers, lying prone on his belly in a small hollow in the hillside, and his neat modern binoculars were trained on the villa. Then, as he watched, the man rolled over on his side and with one hand pulled out a pack of cigarettes and a lighter from the pocket of a tweed jacket that lay on the ground beside him. He put down the binoculars to light a cigarette and put the pack and the lighter beside him as he rolled back on to his stomach. It was the man with the cycle that he had seen the previous evening.

It was just past ten o'clock and too late to be able to warn the girl; she would have left before he could get to the villa or find a telephone. Slowly and cautiously he made his way back to the bridle-path and headed for the stream.

By the time he reached the rock below the waterfall he could see her. She was wearing a blue sweater and jeans, carrying an old-fashioned basket and she was walking across the bridge at the end of the lake. He stood behind the trunk of one of the massive beeches. If she saw him she might wave or call to him. It was ten minutes more before she ap-

128

proached the rock, and as she passed the tree he moved out and put his hand over her mouth and held her with his arm. He pulled her head back roughly so that her ear was near his mouth, and he whispered, 'Don't speak, Anna, it's only me. A man is watching the villa from near the entrance to the woods. Nod if you understand.'

She nodded and he released her, his finger to his lips.

'Give me the basket,' he whispered. 'And follow me as quietly as you can. I'm heading back for the road. He'll be on the top path.'

It was easier going and much quicker, running just below the tree-line in the dead ground, and they met the hill road about a hundred yards from where he had left the car.

'Stay here, Anna, and I'll get the car.'

There was no sign of the man and he released the brakes and let the car roll backwards, steering it on to the road and letting it roll back down the hill to where she was waiting. She slid into the passenger seat and he pushed her head down and let the car go backwards down the hill. When they had turned the sharp bend in the road he switched on the engine and turned the car towards the bottom of the hill. They passed the gates to the villa and then he said, 'OK. Come up for air. We're clear.'

'What on earth's it all about, Hank?'

'There was a man up there watching the villa through binoculars. He was there last night too. I don't like the look of him.'

'Who is he?'

'I've no idea, sweetie, but I'll try and find out. Where shall we go?'

'Where do you want to go?'

He laughed. 'I don't know anywhere. You say.'

'Turn right here. This is the road to Vauvehargues. We'll go there.'

'What's in the pretty basket?'

'Food and wine.'

129

They were both silent until they got to the outskirts of Vauvernargues.

'Is there somewhere I can park the car?'

'It's OK to park anywhere.'

'I mean where it cán't be seen.'

'There is an *auberge*, you can leave it at the back. Over there by the two palms.'

He bought cigarettes at the inn and then they walked almost a mile to a meadow at the foot of a castle, at the edge of the village.

The girl lay back in the lush grass and shaded her eyes from the sun. The meadow was yellow with buttercups and clover and the only clouds in the sky were small, still, high up, and white.

A line of pollarded willows marked the line of a river and on the far side were the wooded slopes of Montagne Ste Victoire.

As he turned to look at the girl she sat up, her legs bent and her head resting on her knees.

'Tell me what you know, Hank.'

'You left the trigger shoe behind in the house of a man named Jansen in one of the Chicago suburbs. The FBI traced it to my store. They said that Jansen had been killed by a .38 slug fired from a PPK, and that they suspected a woman known as Duchamps of having killed him.'

'What did you tell them?'

'Nothing. Absolutely nothing.'

'How did you trace me?'

'Like I said. I cashed in on some CIA debts. You used your real name and passport from Chicago to Toronto because you wanted to use your American Express card. What did you do with the shell by the way?'

'I put it in one of those big metal garbage skips in Toronto.'

'D'you want to talk about it?'

The hazel eyes squinted at him against the sun.

'What do they think was the motive?'

'They've suggested that it could be because he made a pass at you, but they don't really believe it.'

'Why not?'

'It doesn't add up. Women don't carry PPKs around with them on the off-chance that their boy-friends might make a pass at them. If you had thought that you wouldn't have gone. And these days girls don't kill men to cool their ardour. They have other methods.'

'Like what?'

'A tongue-lashing or a kick in the groin.'

'So what did you think? Did you think that I did it?'

'I'm pretty sure you did it. And I'm sure you had a good reason.'

'Tell me a good reason.'

'I've no idea, honey. But if it's good enough for you, it's good enough for me.'

'Are you hungry yet?'

'I'll eat when you're ready.'

'Let's eat then.'

There were sandwiches and fruit and a bottle of red wine, and they had talked of Stanton Falls, and Hank's sister and Tom, and he noticed that she said nothing about herself. As they were repacking the basket she pointed to the château.

'Who do you think that belongs to?'

'I don't know.'

'That was Picasso's home. One of them anyway.' She turned quickly to look at him. And she said softly, 'D'you want to have me, Hank?'

His body cast a shadow across her face as he looked at her.

'I'm a man, honey, so of course I want to have you. But I love you, and that makes it different. And you're in trouble and that makes it even more different.'

'Who says that I'm in trouble?'

'You're on FBI files as a suspect for murder, and you're being watched by a guy who looks a very tough cookie to me.'

'Why should he be tough?'

'God knows. But he is. I can smell it a mile away. He's a killer.'

He saw the surprise and doubt on her face. 'Why should he be watching me?'

Wallace shrugged. 'Only you know that, my love.'

She sighed. 'On the other side of that mountain there's a little village called Puyloubier. There's an inn there, we could stay there tonight.'

'What about your people at the villa? They'll worry.'

'I'll phone them from the inn.'

They walked back for the car and he followed her directions along the mountain road through Pourrieres to Puyloubier.

The small inn stood back from the road, just outside the village, flanked by vineyards and orchards, the afternoon sun bathing it in an orange glow. The girl got out to book them rooms and Wallace drove the car into the small courtyard behind the inn.

He was checking the petrol gauge when he heard someone call his name. He looked around and then up. She was leaning out of a bedroom window. And she was smiling.

'There's only one room, Hank, so we're mister and missus.'

He looked up at her. 'I love you, Anna.'

And he saw the smile fade. She waved and closed the window.

It was a friendly old-fashioned room. Quite large with a magnificent double-bed with polished brass fittings and a duvet covered with a pattern of red roses. There were two comfortable armchairs and a low oak table, smooth and polished from age and use. There was the perfume of mignonette from a box hanging outside the window, and beside the bed was a white china bowl filled with roses.

There was coffee and cups on a tray on the table, and he watched her as she poured out the coffee. She looked at him.

'Cream? Sugar?'

'Both please.'

He sat down facing her and she handed him a cup. Then she leaned back in her chair.

'I'm going to tell you what it's about, Hank, but if you want to make love to me we'd better do that first.'

'Why is that?'

'Because telling you will upset me. And when I've told you what it's about I want you to go back to Stanton Falls. When I've finished what I've got to do I'll come across and see you. We can see what we both think then.'

'Why will telling me upset you?'

She sighed deeply and looked away from him to the window.

'Because it's about my husband. He's dead and I loved him very much. I still do.'

He heard the quaver in her voice and tried to think of something to say. Only common-sense would do. He leaned forward to put down his cup.

'The important thing is to tell me. We can talk about other things another day.'

She turned back to look at him and he saw the brightness of tears in her eyes. She said softly, 'You're a good man, Hank. I don't want to care about anyone, but I do care about you. I did kill the man in Chicago, deliberately, and not because he wanted to sleep with me.'

'Tell me why.'

'He was a German, an ex-SS man. He was one of four men who killed my husband in cold blood.'

'Why should they kill him?'

'He did research work for an organization called the Jewish Documentation Centre in Vienna. He helped them trace Nazi war criminals. The four men belong to a thing called the ODESSA. They were ordered to make revenge killings so that the Documentation Centre would have to close down.'

'How many people did they kill apart from your husband?'

133

'I don't know.'

'Did you know your husband was doing this work?'

'Not until after he was dead.'

'How did you find out?'

'My father-in-law told me and I found their names in his private files.'

'Was your husband a Jew?'

'Yes.'

'Are you?'

'No. I'm not even French. I'm German.'

He tried to keep calm as he absorbed what she had told him. The problems would be psychological and there was little help he could give there. A hot poultice of words to ease her guilt would do its job for a day or a week but it would take months or even years to push the guilt into her subconscious.

'Killing somebody is bound to leave a mark.'

He was aware of the dreadful banality of what he said, but it was the best he could do.

'That's not the problem.'

'What is the problem?'

'You.'

He frowned. 'But I should never talk, girl. I'd never let you down. He deserved to be killed.'

'Not he, Hank, they.'

'I don't understand.'

'I'm going to kill them all. The four of them.'

The room seemed suddenly dark, and involuntarily he looked towards the bedroom window. The sky was still blue and the curtains moved idly in the evening breeze. Eventually he looked back at her.

'Isn't the one enough, Anna, you've made your point with him.'

She shook her head. 'No way, Hank.'

'Who knows about this? Your father-in-law?'

'Nobody knows except you and me.'

'Is this some kind of crazy test to see if I really do love you?'

'No. That's why I want you to go back to Texas and wait for me.'

He shook his head in disbelief. 'While you risk your life trying to kill three more Nazi thugs?'

'Two more.'

His mouth opened to speak and then closed. She saw him swallow before he spoke.

'You've killed another of them?'

'Yes.'

'Oh God.' He hesitated. 'You're not . . .'

He shook his head and she resented the disbelief in his eyes.

'Would you be so shocked if it was a man telling you this?'

'I don't know, Anna. I just don't know.'

'They killed my husband, they killed our unborn child, and they finished my life.'

He reached out and took her hand. It was unresistant, but unresponsive too.

'You didn't tell me about the child.'

'Does it make any difference?'

'It's part of the picture. It's . . .' he spread his arms in a despairing loss of words.

'Will you do as I ask now, and just go back to Stanton Falls?'

The pale blue eyes looked at her face. 'When I came over I knew you were in trouble. I suspected that you had killed a man. I took it for granted that there would be a reason. I came over to help you, not to find out the reason. Now I know the reason it's too unexpected for me to grasp in a few minutes. And just throwing myself in with it would not be a real help. I came to help you and I shall stay to help you. But I'll help you my way when I've had time to sort myself out.'

135

'Have you ever killed a man, Hank?'

'Yes.'

'What had he done?'

He shook his head. 'It won't help, Anna. Forget it.'

'If a man does it then it's OK, yes?'

'Don't press me, love. But there *is* a difference when it is done because of national security.'

He knew it was the wrong thing to say as he said it. And he saw the anger in her eyes.

'They killed my husband, Hank. Coldly, like they killed the Jews in the camps. They killed my baby. What more do they have to do before it is their turn? Nobody else will punish them. They live secure with successful businesses all over the world. No government lifts a finger against them. They live in Germany untouched. Who *will* see justice done?' She clenched her hand and banged the table in fury. 'I will. An eye for an eye, a life for a life. They're savages, and they should be dealt with as they dealt with their victims. Without mercy.'

He looked at her flushed face, the blazing eyes, the determined mouth; and tried to understand. And failed.

'D'you know who the other two are?'

'Yes.'

'Do you know where they live?'

'Yes.'

'Tell me where.'

'One is in London, just outside; and the last one is in Portugal.'

He took her hand again, in both of his.

'You order dinner for us while I go for a walk. I'll be back in about ten minutes.'

She sighed deeply. 'All right. But nothing, absolutely nothing, will make me change my mind.'

He walked, oblivious to his surroundings, mile after mile, his mind in turmoil. Although he could understand her motives and her need for revenge, he found it difficult to believe that she had actually murdered two men and intended killing two more. She was too attractive, too ordinary to do such things. No matter what she said or thought it was a man's reaction and if it had to be done at all it should be done by a man. He stopped by a stone wall and looked across at the high ridge of the mountain. It looked like some headless monster in the setting sun. An evil omen.

He turned and walked back towards the inn. He looked at his watch. He had already been away nearly an hour.

The girl pulled her chair to the window but she saw nothing as she looked out. If only he hadn't found her. If only he wasn't the kind of man he was. If only he had been as other men are, happy to have her body, and leave it at that. If only she didn't like him.

She didn't want to have to justify what she was doing to anybody. Not even herself. It was a route to follow. A set of things to be done. It diverted her mind from her emptiness and sadness. And the morality of what she was doing had never entered her mind. It wasn't an issue. But all that security seemed to have gone. By the time her training with him was over she had admired him and liked him. Like Paul, he had an inner security; but despite that he listened to what she said as if it mattered, to be weighed and considered. Her initial irritation when he had appeared on the hillside had bordered on open anger. Anger at what seemed like interference. But it had ebbed away as she talked with him. It was like meeting an old friend, a fellow veteran from some forgotten war. But lying below the surface was that vague feeling of disloyalty to a dead man. She liked the American's affection for her, and subconsciously welcomed his desire. If there had been a dozen empty rooms at the inn she would have wanted to sleep in his bed. She had looked at her body as she dressed that morning and as she slid her long legs into the black lacy briefs she knew that she was putting them on for him to take off at the edge of the woods.

And now it was all spoilt. He didn't understand. He sat in judgement. He sympathized but didn't really care. He

137

wanted *her*, not her mourning. He wanted to drag her into a new life away from the old. He wouldn't join her, she would have to join him.

She looked quickly towards the door as she heard footsteps in the corridor. She watched as he closed the door, leaning back against it, looking at her, his tanned face pale, his eyes concerned.

'I've thought about it, Anna. I know what we must do.'

She sat silent and unmoving for a moment and then sighed.

'Tell me,' she said.

'I'll kill them for you. Leave it to me.'

He saw the tears build in her eyes and then overflow, her lips trembling as she tried to speak. He waited in the dim light of the room. Waiting for her to respond.

It seemed a long time before she spoke. She said softly, 'Take me to bed, Hank. Make love to me.'

Chapter Sixteen

They hardly heard the thunder or saw the room blaze with summer lightning through the night. And it was the false dawn when they finally lay, wide awake, but temporarily at peace. Their mental tensions seemed to have been assuaged in the releasing of their physical tensions. It seemed that now they could talk, discuss, without having to tear down the barriers of separateness and privacy.

She talked about Paul and their life together, and her days at the villa; and she made him talk about the woman he would only refer to as 'Tom's mother'. And for the first time in months she felt sympathy for another human being.

There were the first glimmerings of the day's sun when he brought them back to earth.

'Will you wait at the villa until I come back?'

'No. I want to do it another way. I'm still going to do it myself. It's my thing. My destiny. But I'll come back to you.'

'I'm afraid for you, love. Deeply afraid.'

'You trained me well. I can do it.'

'It's not only that that makes me afraid.'

'What then?'

'You won't be angry if I explain?'

'Tell me anyway.'

'You pay a price when you kill someone. It's a different price for different people. It doesn't matter whether the killing is just or unjust, you still pay the price. You don't necessarily pay immediately; it may be years later when you have almost forgotten what happened. But you pay. And you always seem to pay when you can least afford it.'

'So how would I pay?'

'God knows, my love, there's a dozen currencies you can

pay in. But pay you will. You might end up tainted and infected by the very people you hate. A fellow victim. A fellow killer, with the same indifference to what had happened. Or perhaps the opposite, and haunted by what you had done.'

'How have you paid for your killings, Hank?'

'I don't know, honey, I'm not sure we ever do know. Maybe we pay without recognizing that we're paying. I hide behind my fragile piece of armour; that I was ordered to do it. It was official and it saved many people's lives. I've seen others pay.'

'What happened?'

'Two suicides, an alcoholic, two, maybe three, drug addicts, and boatloads of broken marriages.'

'That's all the more reason for me to do it.'

'I don't see it that way.'

'I believe in what I'm doing. That's my armour. You would only be doing it for me.'

'Honey, you're gonna be like the man on the high-wire.'

'Tell me.'

'He goes along fine until he looks down. One day you're gonna look down.'

'And you'll be there to catch me.'

He kissed her. 'You betcha. Now it's sleep time.' And he patted her bottom as she twined herself uncomfortably, but lovingly, around him.

They breakfasted in their room and it was nearly eleven. As she sipped her coffee she said, 'Can I suggest a compromise, Hank?'

'Sure.'

'Let me carry on as I had planned but you come with me as moral support.'

'I'll do whatever you want, honey. If that's what you want, that's the way we go.'

Every part of him knew it was crazy. But he wanted to please so he really had no choice. He had a real relationship with her now and he didn't want to upset its fragile balance by arguing or disagreeing except for some practical reason. There would be other times when he could reiterate the moral dangers.

'Tell me what you know about the two men that we've got to deal with.'

'One's named Walther Müller, he's got a photographic shop near London. The other is a Wilhelm Trommer, he's a fruit farmer in Portugal.'

'What else do you know?'

'Nothing.'

'No photographs or background material?'

'No.'

'How about we go across to London and have a look at Müller?'

'When shall we go?'

'Tonight. After dark, if there's a suitable plane.'

'Why after dark?'

'I'm thinking of the guy who's watching the villa. There's just a chance he could be police.'

'What makes you think that? I thought you said he looked like a killer.'

'He does, but he's got an air of authority like he was used to surveillance. With two of their men gone the ODESSA people might have tipped off the police. Did you pick up the shells in Amsterdam?'

'No. I panicked. I had to fire twice. He took me by surprise.'

'If the ODESSA have connected the two deaths the police could use the two slugs to confirm that it was the same gun. How did you get the PPK through the security checks?'

'I stripped it and put it under the frame of a typewriter.'

'Not bad. I'll take you back to the villa now and pick you up tonight at ten. If there's a plane to London we'll take it, otherwise we'll fly to Paris and on to London tomorrow.'

'OK.'

'Why don't you tell your father-in-law about the man in the

woods. He could make a routine complaint to the police.'

'I'll see what he says. What did he look like?'

'He cycles up there. An old bike. Late fifties but dark hair, slightly wavy, about five foot ten or eleven. Was wearing casual clothes, a dark green shirt and brown slacks. Typical camouflage colours. Quite good looking.'

'What made you think he was a killer?'

'His eyes, and when I passed him the first time he moved over and passed me on my left side.'

'What's wrong with that?'

'Nothing. But when I saw him the next time he was holding the binoculars in his left hand. He held his lighter in his left hand too. He moved over on the path the first time because he's left-handed, and it gave him an advantage to be on my left. He did it without thinking. It was a reflex.'

'Shall I book us on the plane?'

'No. I'll do that. I need to tie up the timing.'

He dropped her at the villa gate and arranged for her to phone him at the *pension* at four.

They stayed overnight in Paris, and landed at Gatwick after lunch. Wallace bought a street map and guide and they studied it while they had coffee in the cafeteria. Croydon was barely covered in the street guide It was well out of London. They checked at the British Airways counter about an hotel, and were given a name and telephone number.

The hotel was in Sanderstead, the Selsdon Park Hotel. They parked the hire-car outside the front entrance and took in their bags, and booked two adjoining rooms.

Wallace sat on the girl's bed running his finger slowly down the list of names and addresses in the Yellow Pages.

'There's no Müller. There's a Miller. Maybe that's him.'

'It's the English equivalent name anyway.'

'It's Miller Photographics, The Parade, South Croydon.'

He looked up at her. 'I'll go down and look it over, you have a rest.'

The shop was double-fronted, its windows crammed full of expensive equipment. There was a regular flow of customers and two assistants who were being kept pretty busy.

The door bell clanged as he pushed the door open. He stood waiting as the two assistants served the customers who were ahead of him. Eventually it was his turn. The red-haired young man looked amiable enough.

'I'd like to speak to Mr Miller if he's about.'

'I'm afraid Mr Miller's not available, but Mr Evans, the manager is here.'

'Maybe I could speak to Mr Evans then.'

'What name is it, sir?'

'Abercrombie.'

'And what is it about, sir?'

'I'm from *Modern Photography* magazine in the US of A.'

The red-haired boy smiled and shook his head.

'He won't see advertising reps without appointments, sir. He's very touchy about it.'

'I'm not selling advertising, son, I'm doing a review of British photo shops for American visitors to the UK.'

'I'll just check, sir.'

He came back a few minutes later.

'Mr Evans'll see you in a few moments, sir.'

Wallace stood looking at the lenses in the glass cases on the wall, and putting together his questions. When Evans came out he was a rather solemn-looking man in his early forties and he showed Wallace into the tiny back office, its desk piled with leaflets, invoices and cardboard cartons.

'Sit down, Mr Abercrombie. Rod tells me you're from *Modern Photography*.'

'That's right, Mr Evans. I'm doing just a brief summary of photo dealers around London for a piece we're doing on travel photography in Europe.'

'And how can I help you?'

143

'Maybe I'd better get the basics first. I assume from the name that the business is owned by a Mr Miller. Is that correct?'

'Yes. Mr Walter Miller is the sole owner. 'He's not available at the moment.'

'When will he be back? I could call tomorrow.'

'He's on holiday I'm afraid. It could be another couple of weeks before he's back. I'm not sure when he returns.'

Wallace smiled. 'I hope he took his camera with him like it says on the poster in the shop.'

Evans laughed but with no great enthusiasm, and Wallace guessed that Evans was merely a senior employee. He did what he was told.

'He's a great photographic enthusiast, Mr Abercrombie. He says you can't sell photo-equipment if you don't know how to use it.'

'A good precept, Mr Evans. I'll make a note of that for the editorial. Have you got a good photograph of the premises I could use?'

Evans reached out for a box-file and folded back the lid. It was crammed with photographs. He sorted through the heap.

'We had one taken a couple of months ago when we did a special Olympus display. Ah, yes, here it is.'

Wallace studied the photograph. 'That's fine, can I keep this print?'

'Certainly.'

'Now what about a photograph of the owner, Mr Miller. By the way, how does he style himself – Walter or Wally?'

'I think he prefers Walter, Mr Abercrombie. But I don't think I've got a portrait. I'll have a look.'

He lifted out the pile of prints. Wallace waited a few seconds.

'Maybe I could have a look through and see if there's anything else we could use.'

He reached for part of the pile and went through it slowly.

144

There were photographs of special window displays, counter-displays, publicity prints of pieces of equipment, and a few glamour shots of pretty girls. A picture of a group of amateurs, a model in a bikini and an array of studio lights. And then a picture that made Wallace's blood run cold. It was a Polaroid colour print of a pretty girl, nude and sitting on a draped dais. A man was standing by a studio light facing the camera, his hand held out, pointing, to emphasize something he was saying. His mouth caught open by the flash as he spoke. It was the man he had seen watching the villa and he had no doubt now who he was. He held out the print to Evans.

'Is that the boss by any chance?'

Evans twisted his head to look at the print. 'Yes that's him. But I'd like to find a better one if I can.'

Five minutes later Evans smiled. 'That's the one I had in mind. I think he'd prefer that one.'

Müller was in a dark suit, leaning on the glass counter, pointing his finger at a camera as if explaining its virtues to the red-haired shop assistant. The typed caption on the back said 'Mr W. Miller explains the sales points of the Canon A1 camera to one of his assistants, Rodney Elmes'.

'Yes I agree, Mr Evans, this is the one we should use. May I have this copy?'

'Certainly.'

'Where's Mr Miller vacationing?'

'I don't really know. I'm not sure whether it was business or pleasure. He went off at very short notice.'

'He must think a lot of you, Mr Evans, to leave you in charge.'

'I've been with him for ten years now.'

Wallace talked about the lines they handled, their studio and processing facilities and then he stood up. The two prints in his jacket pocket.

'It's good of you to give me your time, Mr Evans. Give Mr Miller my best regards when you contact him.'

'It's a pleasure, Mr Abercrombie, when will it appear?'

'We do a round-up in our December issue. I guess it will be in that.'

The hotel was one of those typically English country-house style buildings. Overgrown with ivy, Virginia creeper beginning to turn red around the mullioned windows and armorial bearings carved on a stone escutcheon over the arched doorway.

There were guests in evening dress arriving for some function, and for a moment he envied them their normality. The carpeted stairs creaked under his feet as he slowly made his way to the first floor.

On the journey from Müller's shop he had tried to work out how he could get over to the girl that she was in real danger without it seeming that he was trying to scare her off her plan. And how could he convince her, without saying the actual words, that he was now quite sure what her payment to fate would be. And that it was almost certain that he would pay along with her.

She was asleep on the bed when he went into her room. The leaded windows were open and he looked out across the golf course that provided the hotel's landscape. It was finding the first words that was difficult. And then with a flood of relief he knew what to do. It might bring him an ally.

He sat reading that morning's paper as he waited for her to wake. It was almost an hour before she stirred. She opened her eyes, rubbed them and stretched out her arms.

'Any luck, Hank?'

'Yes and no. That was his place, but he's away on a business trip. I suggest I take you back to the villa and then we'll go down to Portugal and have a look at Herr Trommer.'

'When's Müller coming back?'

'They don't know. They thought a couple of weeks maybe.'

He went into his own room to bath and change, then

collected her and took her down to dinner in the restaurant.

There was an orchestra and a few couples dancing and when they had finished their consommé he took her hand and walked her on to the small dance floor because they were playing 'Manhattan' and the girl singer was saying '. . . and tell me what street compares with Mott Street in July . . .' And impulsively he said, 'Where do you want to live when it's all over, Anna?'

She looked up quickly at his face. 'You know, Hank, I've never thought about what happens when it's over. Not for me. Not for us. There were these things to do and then a blank. There's Tom and your sister, so I guess it should be Stanton Falls.'

He nodded. 'We'll see. We'll work something out.'

She looked up smiling. 'God, it would be wonderful to have a nice reason to be alive.'

There was a big harvest moon and they walked, after dinner, across the slope of the eighteenth hole and sat on the edge of a bunker.

'Will your father-in-law mind about me?'

'No. He'll understand. He's a marvellous man. He'll be glad for me.'

'Can I meet him when we get back?'

'Of course. You'll like him.'

After they had gone back upstairs he walked through into his own bedroom for his pyjamas, and as he hung up his jacket he looked again at the photograph of Müller. The camera was held in his right hand and he was pointing with his left, which a right-handed man would have found awkward. The flash had given a sharp, clear image of his face. The smile was contrived, but that could be because he knew he was posing for a photograph, but that wasn't what had put the look in his eyes. They were animal eyes, alert and watchful, aware of all that was happening. His hands were big and strong and there was the lift of muscle just above his wrist where his coat sleeve was pulled back. Even the smile was arrogant and knowing. He tucked the photograph back

147

in his jacket. The girl wouldn't have stood a chance against Müller.

She was sitting on the bed when he went back into her room. Her open handbag lay beside her, and a photograph lay alongside it on the bed-cover. And she was crying, sobbing, with her hands to her face.

He sat down on the bed and reached for the photograph. He thought it would be a picture of her husband. For long moments his eyes absorbed the line of women and children, the big defeated eyes in the half-starved faces. The hopelessness. The ragged Stars of David roughly sewn on sleeves. The cattle marked for slaughter. Despite his feelings for the girl, and compassion for her unhappiness, he had seen her need for such an elaborate revenge as an exaggerated, neurotic display of a temporarily unsettled mind. Out of character and the product of a sad, brooding sickness. For the first time he realized that it was far more than that. This photograph was a kind of talisman, that consecrated what she was doing. Even as the Nazis had said that the ends justified the means. It was more than revenge for her husband's death. He was a Jew and this was a revenge on their behalf too. And she was German, striking back at the maniacs who had given a whole nation their own imprint of brutality. He sighed, because although it made her actions the more understandable, he knew that with this double motivation there would be no chance of diverting her by argument or persuasion.

He moved the photograph and the handbag to one side and put his arm round her shoulders.

There was nothing to say that would comfort her. Nothing that he could bring himself to say.

Chapter Seventeen

Pierre Simon had been charming but wary of the American. The girl had not been able to explain how Wallace had helped her and the Frenchman wondered why his daughter-in-law should have visited a small town in Texas. He sensed too that the American was critical of him in some way. Watchful, over-aware of everything he said. Probing without seeming to probe, a kind of low-key interrogation.

They slept in separate bedrooms, neither of them was the one that had once been his son's.

It was the third night, after Anna had gone up to bed, and the two men were drinking whisky alone, that he decided to probe a little himself.

'I thought Anna looked a little less well, Mr Wallace, than when she left.'

Wallace turned his head to look at his host.

'You're right. M'sieur Simon. She *is* less well.'

'I think we could be Hank and Pierre, don't you?'

'I'd appreciate that. Maybe between us we could help her.'

'You have something in mind?'

'Yes.' He looked at Pierre's brown eyes. 'Do you have any idea what she's been doing these last two months?'

'None at all I'm afraid.'

'Not even a vague suspicion?'

Pierre frowned. 'Suspicion. I'm in no position to entertain suspicions of Anna. Suspicions of what?'

'Anything.'

'I'm afraid you're talking in terms I don't understand, Hank.'

'Are you on her side?'

'Totally.'

'No matter what she might have done?'

Pierre Simon nodded. 'No matter what.'

'She's in danger of her life, Pierre.'

'From whom?'

'From the ODESSA.'

Simon shook his head. 'When they killed my son that was the end of it. They will know that she had nothing to do with his work.'

Wallace watched the Frenchman's face carefully as he spoke. 'Maybe they know that she knows the names of the men responsible for her husband's death.'

'She doesn't know. How could she know?'

'*You* know who they are. Don't you?'

'True.'

Wallace leaned forward and said softly, 'Why did you leave your office open, and the keys in the filing cabinets?'

Simon frowned. 'I don't understand. What has my office got to do with all this?'

'That's where she got their names, Pierre.'

Pierre Simon closed his eyes. 'My God. Oh, my God.'

'You didn't know? You didn't mean it to happen?'

The Frenchman sighed as he looked at Wallace.

'Of course not. It would do no good. The police – governments – they won't lift a finger.'

'Two of them are already dead, Pierre.'

'Dead?'

'Yes. Anna killed them.'

The silence, the tension in the room was almost unbearable as the two men looked at each other. Pierre Simon shook his head.

'She could never kill, that girl.'

'She shot them both with a Walther PPK. She came to me in Texas. Told me she was a writer doing research. She paid me to train her to shoot. I gave her the gun when she had finished her training.'

'And the police?'

'One man was killed in Chicago, the other in Amsterdam.

There is no reason for either police force to connect the two crimes.'

'The ODESSA will tell them.'

'Never. How do they explain why they were killed. The ODESSA keep well away from the police. No. They'll deal with Anna themselves.'

Wallace saw that Pierre Simon was devastated by what he had been told. He would need time to absorb it. Time to recover. But there was one more thing that had to be done.

'Pierre.'

'Yes.'

'I can look after Anna, but there is something I want you to do.'

'Tell me.'

'She loved your son Paul. She is obsessed now with her plans. She sees herself as an avenging angel. Not only for Paul but for the Jews. She intends killing the other two. If I try to persuade her not to do this I say it as an outsider. An outsider who loves her. And that makes me suspect. She thinks I don't understand how she feels. But I do. But I also know that some day she is going to realize what she has done.'

There were a few moments of silence before Pierre spoke.

'And what has she done?'

'She has joined her enemies. She is judge, jury and executioner just as they were. She doesn't know it and she may never recognize it. But she is going to pay a terrible price for this. Already she has gone a long way down that path. When she has killed two more she will be doomed. Nobody can save her then, we can only wait with her until . . . until the debt is called.'

'Are you some kind of policeman, Hank?'

'I was once in the CIA. I run a sports goods store in a small town in Texas now. I'm divorced, and I've got a son aged seventeen.'

'Are you going to marry her?'

'If she'll have me.'

151

'What do you want me to do?'

'Talk to her. Try to persuade her that she shouldn't go on with her plans.'

'I'll do my best, but . . .' He spread his hands and let them drop, hopelessly.

'I need to take her away from here, Pierre. They're already after her. Did you tell the police about the man in the woods?'

'What man?'

'Twice before we left I saw a man watching the villa from the woods. The last time he was watching through binoculars. When we were in England I found out who he was. He's the man she was going to kill next. Walther Müller. He's here to kill her. I asked her to get you to report a trespasser to the police before I knew who he was.'

'She didn't mention it to me.'

'*She* doesn't know that he's Müller, and I don't want her to know. And now I'll deal with him myself.'

The old man's drawn, white face looked like a caricature of the face he had shown earlier that evening. He was rocking gently from side to side in tension. 'My God, what a night, Hank. What a terrible, terrible night.'

'Leave it to me, Pierre, and I'll straighten it out one way or another, but try and persuade her. I'm afraid for her.'

'And what about you, my boy, what about you?'

'Don't worry about me, sir. I'll survive.'

Pierre managed a faint smile. 'You would have liked my Paul, and he would have liked you.'

Wallace recognized the pathetic gesture.

'I already like him, Pierre.'

The girl was asleep when he went into her room. The photograph on the small table at the side of the bed, propped against the bedside lamp.

Wallace sat on the small mound that commanded the bridle-path into the woods from just after nine o'clock. The stand of young willows gave him almost complete cover, and his face and hands were smeared with mud. The midges and mosquitoes that hung around him in clouds would have worried an expert if he were expecting trouble. By mid-day the sweat was pouring down his face and his clothes stuck coldly and clamily to his body. He moved his feet from time to time, slowly and carefully flexing his ankles. Patiently and imperceptibly he moved each part of his body from time to time. Then he saw him.

He was wheeling the bicycle and looking to his left as he made his way up the bridle-path. He was in the same green shirt and brown slacks, sweating from his ride. He stopped, sitting with his backside against the cross-bar as he wiped his face with a khaki handkerchief. And under the fat back-side Wallace saw the leather gun-case. It was a case for a game gun, but he guessed that it was a target rifle that was inside. Then as Müller moved on, Wallace heard him humming softly to himself. It sounded as if Müller was very sure of himself, and that might help.

Müller unstrapped the gun case and leaned it against one of the trees while he lifted the cycle into the middle of a clump of rhododendrons. He tugged and wrestled it into place and then stood back to check that it was well-hidden.

Seemingly satisfied, he walked back for the gun-case and slung the strap over his shoulder. Wallace looked at his watch. It was two thirty and the sun would be lighting the patio like a film-set. As Müller pushed through the bushes Wallace stood up quietly. He froze as Müller looked back over his shoulder towards the entrance to the woods. Then he went on. Wallace bent low and ran across the pathway and took cover behind the first line of trees. It would be better to take him before he settled down, while the noise of his own movements was still in his ears and his mind was concentrated on checking the gun.

Wallace moved forward cautiously from tree to tree as he heard Müller crashing through the dry undergrowth. When Müller stood at the edge of the woods looking out Wallace was barely twenty feet away from him. He went down on his elbows and knees, and crawled slowly forward. Müller was sliding out a telescopic sight from the case and looking towards the villa. Wallace froze while Müller looked through the sight. He was no more than ten feet away now. Müller unslung the gun case and started unbuckling the top strap. Ten feet was not going to be enough when he had the gun out, and Wallace stooped quickly in the ferns to find a good sized stone. As he stood up he pitched it to Müller's right, and hurled himself forward. His body took Müller square, as he went down sideways Müller's feet came up and locked Wallace's leg. The German was lying awkwardly across the roots of a beech tree and he stumbled as he tried to get to his feet. Wallace wrenched his foot free and lashed at the German's groin. Despite his scream of pain the German's head smashed into Wallace's face, blinding him for vital seconds, and as his eyes cleared he saw Müller dive for the gun case and try to shake the rifle free. As Wallace went at him again the German crouched to take the rush, his hands dropping the case. Then they were on the ground, their hands clawing for a hold. The German's hand slipping on the sweat as it gripped Wallace's jaw. For a fleeting second Wallace saw Müller's throat through a curtain of sweat, and he chopped at it with all his strength and felt the pain shoot up his arm. Müller's chest was heaving as he tried desperately to draw breath through his injured windpipe, and Wallace smashed his hand across his throat again and again, then pressed with both thumbs as Müller's heels drummed on the ground and his hands clawed weakly at Wallace's wrists.

Long after Müller was still, and the woods were silent, Wallace crouched there, his hands on the dead man's throat. When, eventually, he stumbled to his feet, the earth seemed to tilt and move and he fell forward on his knees. There was blood down his shirt and on his hands, and the little finger of his right hand stuck out at a crazy angle. There was blood in his mouth and he could feel a loose tooth under his tongue.

The walk down the valley and up the hill to the villa

garden was a nightmare of leaden feet and tortured lungs. He was almost at the blue door when it opened and the girl ran out.

'What's happened, Hank? You've been hurt.'

'Fetch Pierre.'

'What happened?'

'Fetch Pierre,' he said again. And then he fainted.

Pierre Simon was gently washing his face, telling him to lie still.

'Müller's body, Pierre ... back in the woods ... I've got to ... I've got to bury it ... quickly ...'

'I'll see to that, Hank. Jean-Louis and I will deal with it. Don't talk. I've sent for the doctor.'

'No ... that's impossible ...' He could hear his distorted words, he was talking as dumb people talk. Just sounds, not words.

When he came to again he was in bed, and Pierre was sitting beside him. There was a bandage round his jaw and across one eye. He couldn't speak.

'The doctor's fixed your jaw. It wasn't broken. It was unhinged. He's set your finger. We've dealt with our friend. I'll tell you more tomorrow. Meantime you rest. The doctor was from Aix. A Jew. He was in Mauthausen concentration camp. He knows nothing but in any case he won't talk.'

Pierre Simon sat with him until he slept.

They sat together on the patio and there was the smell of lavender from the garden. There had been one of those violent Provençal autumn storms during the night but now the sky was clear again and the sun shone as if it were the height of summer.

The girl was stroking his hand where it lay on her leg.

'Why won't either of you tell me what happened?'

'There's no point, sweetheart, just forget it.'

She sighed with exasperation. 'You men.'

'I saw a map on your bed this morning. A tourist map of the Algarve.'

155

'You don't have to be involved, Hank. I can't just wait. I want to get it done. There's still the man in England.'

'Did Pierre talk to you?'

'Yes. But he's an old man. He exaggerated the problems.' She smiled at him. 'Apart from that, I've heard the theme before, from you. It's those bastards who are going to do the paying not me.'

It almost seemed as if their warnings to her had only made her even more determined.

Pierre Simon had shown him where Müller's body had been buried near the waterfall where the soil was deep before it met the limestone ridge.

They had kept the rifle for him to check. It was a .22 heavy barrel 1411 by Anschütz, with a palmrest and a Kassnar zoom-scope with a rubber eyecup. The kind of rifle that took all the Olympic gold medals. Wallace had wrapped it in oily rags and plastic film and it had been laid in the rubble before eight inches of concrete were poured over an extension to the conservatory.

He sat watching as she struck with her arm and fist. After the third time he called her over.

'You're not doing it as if you mean it, girl. It's not a game or an exercise. Karate is violent. Look at this.'

He held out his arm and fist. 'Look, a straight line, the back of my fist in line with the forearm. The fist clenched. Show me again how you clench your fist.'

He watched, and then stopped her. 'Fold your little finger first, *then* the others, and then lock them in position with your thumb. That's it . . . thumb right under . . . now lock hard. Do it again, slowly. OK. Now show me the "*tsuki*" again.'

He had made her wear only a short skirt and her bra so that he could watch the sinews and muscles of her arms and shoulders.

He called out as she struck. 'With all your body, shoulder

156

lower. Imagine a knife in your hand. Again . . . that's better
. . . stop.'

She stood there panting, swinging her right arm to take
away the pain.

'Keep your mouth closed and that shoulder down, just
those two things will show your opponent that you're frightened. Your legs should be firm and your buttocks taut. Show
me again.'

She never complained at his driving criticism, she accepted it and tried to absorb all he said.

Each day since the bandages had come off he had taken
her down to the meadow beyond the lake, and there, in the
half-circle of umbrella pines he taught her how to defend
herself. He tried not to think what would have happened if
she had tackled Müller on her own.

He walked over to her and stood facing her.

'D'you remember the "*yoko-geri*", Anna?'

'Yes.'

'OK. We'll try that. And remember the three movements
must flow into one.'

He struck with clenched fist and rigid bent arm, and he
barely glimpsed her knee coming up and the sideways stroke
of her heel that took him in the chest. Before he could recover she came forward with an '*oie-tsuki*'. Her fist took
him in the throat and she placed one leg behind his as she
turned her body, and he was on his back with her foot
swinging for his groin. He took her foot in both hands and
twisted until she fell and was still.

'That was first-class, Anna.' He panted. 'Really good.
That's enough for a bit. For me anyway.'

They sat in the shade of the trees, eating the salad from
the hamper, and he was quietly pleased with her progress.
Day after day for three weeks he had turned her defence into
attack. Making her treat each '*kata*' as a matter of life or
death.

When the afternoon heat began to ebb he set her working

157

again, to strengthen those vulnerable areas under her arms and down her sides. They walked back towards the waterfall and washed their bodies in the cold, pure torrent of the stream. When they sat drying themselves in the sun he asked her to describe how she had gone about her reconnaissance of Jansen and Stein. He listened carefully, asking questions only when it was essential. When she had finished he turned his head to look at her.

'You realize that because of what has happened to Stein and Jansen anyone else will be expecting an attack. It's going to be much harder from now onwards.'

'It's easier if you're a woman, Hank.'

'It was before. It's a disadvantage now. They'll have got alongside the police in Chicago and Amsterdam, and they'll have heard that in both cases the only suspect is a woman. They'll have a description too. The Chicago police had a very accurate description of you.'

'What are you trying to tell me?'

'That from now onwards everything is planned very carefully. We do a real reconnaissance. And we don't rush things.'

'OK. Who shall I tackle first, Müller or Trommer?'

'We don't even know that Müller is back from his trip yet. Better make it Trommer.' He didn't feel guilty as he deceived her, it was for her own good.

'Do you know Portugal at all?'

'I've been to Lisbon once, but that's all. Do you?'

She shook her head. 'I'm afraid not.'

There was virtually nothing on the Algarve in the library at Aix. A couple of uninformative guide books and no maps. A phone call to Paris indicated that there were no official maps of Portugal. Not even in Portugal.

The planning would have to be done on the spot.

Chapter Eighteen

It was a small office and even without the two smokers it wasn't suitable for long meetings. The five of them had sat round the table for three hours and Inspector van Laan had a lunch appointment that he didn't want to miss.

'Well, we either send de Vries on his wild goose chase or we close the case. For the time being anyway.'

Zeeman from the Public Prosecutor's office was back to square one, and van Laan sighed and leaned back in his chair with his eyes closed.

'The German Embassy in the Hague have made inquiries, the media are still chewing at it. And all we can say is that the police are still actively pursuing their investigation.'

'My dear Zeeman, it's the end of a fine hot summer, the bloody newspapers have nothing to write about so they speculate on the murder of a German. Is it revenge for war-time misdeeds? Is it political? Is it the Baader-Meinhof striking at a German capitalist pig. You know, and I know, that if Stein had been a greengrocer, German or whatever, there wouldn't have been a line in the newspaper. But he was rich, and a queer, and he got shot, so it's a story. The German Embassy hadn't raised a whisper until the bloody newspapers kept the story on the boil. Queers are always quarrelling, breaking up, flouncing out on one another. Some jealous queer does him in. The art dealers all hated him. We've got a dozen anonymous letters on his file asking where he got the money from to start up. Maybe it's one of them.'

'But you've got clues, Inspector.'

'Oh shit. We've got two shell cases and one used slug. Ballistics can confirm that they were fired from a Walther PPK. They also confirm from the pattern of the scoring that the pistol had probably not fired more than two thousand shots since new. There's probably not more than twenty thousand PPKs that fit that description. We also have our friend de Vries. He knows of a girl who was a visitor to Amsterdam in the two weeks before Stein was shot. She was often in Stein's company, and is known to have visited the farm twice with him. The farm manager and his wife confirm this. They confirm that she was there on the day he was shot. The same day she checks out of her hotel and that's the last we hear of her.'

'We've got a description of her?'

Van Laan sat upright in his chair, his arms on the table as he leaned forward towards Zeeman.

'Holy Jesus, have you read the description. Dark hair, medium height, very attractive, big tits, long legs, was heard speaking German, French and English and looks a bit like Jane Fonda.' He leaned back in disgust. 'I could find you thirty whores answering that description down just one side of Rembrandtsplein.'

'But we have a police officer who actually saw her, is familiar with her.'

'Too bloody familiar if you ask me. Have you seen his second statement. I quote. "It is my impression that this young woman would be unlikely to have committed this crime or any act of violence." My God, it's the ones with the big brown eyes and the little girl voices that stick knives in six foot sailors.'

'So you want me to tell the Director that you feel unable to co-operate?'

Van Laan sighed theatrically. 'No, Zeeman, I don't want you to tell the Director that I won't co-operate. I want you to tell him that I think it's a waste of time, but if he wants us to do it then I'll put de Vries on to it right away. But . . .' And he held up a thick forefinger. 'But it comes out of the DPP's funds, not police funds.'

'He's already agreed that.'

'OK. You send me written confirmation and I'll press the button.'

'Within the hour, Inspector, I assure you.'

Van Laan looked at his watch. It was 1.45. She wouldn't have waited.

He saw the others out of his office and reached for the phone.

'Send de Vries in, and get me *De Goudenleeuw*.'

He waved de Vries to a seat, the phone still to his ear.

'The Golden Lion? ... yes ... Inspector van Laan, is Mevrouw Lorentz still there ... I see ... ah, yes ... thank you.' And he crashed the receiver back on its cradle.

'As usual, you're causing trouble, de Vries. Anyway, is your passport up to date?'

'Yes, sir.'

'Visas OK for France, Germany, England, etcetera?'

'They're all Common Market sir, no visas needed. It depends on where etcetera might be.'

Van Laan glanced at him, biting back the words on his tongue.

'On the instructions of the Public Prosecutor's Office you will trace the whereabouts of the mysterious Mam'selle Duchamps. When you have found her you will not interrogate her or approach her, but you will contact this office for further instructions. Understood?'

'Yes, sir. Where do I draw funds?'

'See Pieter Zeeman, he'll fix you up.'

'Right, sir.'

'And, de Vries.'

'Sir.'

'Learn how to give a proper description of a suspect. There's a list in the Promotion Handbook.'

De Vries opened his mouth to speak, saw the look on van Laan's face, and closed the door quietly behind him.

Nobody would have thought from his treatment of his subordinate that van Laan considered him an excellent detective. Despite de Vries' university education and his chamber music, van Laan knew that the young man had that ability

161

that all good detectives have of bridging the gaps in the evidence. He could find those small nuts and bolts that could join up disparate bits of apparently unrelated evidence, the bits that made a chain out of half a dozen links. He had asked him once how he did it, and after due reflection de Vries had said solemnly and seriously that he thought he had a criminal mind.

Jan de Vries picked up the money, the traveller's cheques and the travel pass, and walked to his apartment.

He packed a bag, tidily, using the corners for his shaving kit. On top of his clothes he put a miniature score of the Bruch Violin Concerto. The one in G minor.

He sat on the bed for a moment, his eyes closed in thought. He knew where he was going, and he knew how it would end, but he wasn't sure about the bit in between.

Van Laan would have been shocked to know that de Vries had spent the three months waiting to see if he had graduated in trying to decide whether he would become a policeman or a priest. To have considered becoming a policeman would have sat quite easily with a final decision to be a priest. But the reverse had far less logic. There were times even now, when Jan de Vries turned a blind eye or a deaf ear to things done or said, because he abrogated to himself things, decisions, that belonged more to his seniors or perhaps to the country. Policemen are allowed 'discretion', it almost said so in the handbooks. Ignore offensive remarks from bad drivers when you stopped them if they were accompanied by a girl. But nowhere was there even a faint hint that policemen's discretion extended to ignoring evidence. And that was what he had been doing for the last two weeks. He sighed quietly and stood up. With a last look round the room he picked up his bag and left.

The scale of travel charges meant that it took him two and a half days to get to Aix and a call from the kiosk outside the Post Office had provided the first bad news. Madame Simon was not available, not in residence and her present address was not known.

He had shown his warrant at the *préfecture* and asked for their help in finding a possible witness who was in no way involved with a crime. She was not at the villa, he told them, and the servants couldn't give an address. Could *they*, perhaps, use their influence?

They recommended a pension near the *préfecture*, and he waited there in his room. They phoned early the next day to say that they had spoken discreetly to Monsieur Simon but he had not been able to help them. They were almost certain that he was being evasive. They would make other inquiries.

He waited four days before there was any more information. Discreet inquiries had been made, and it seemed that Madame Simon and Mr Wallace, who had a United States passport, had both boarded a flight to Faro, via Paris, nearly a week ago.

De Vries was disappointed about the Mr Wallace bit. But maybe there was an explanation. He phoned van Laan who gave him permission to proceed to Portugal. But there would be no contact made with Madame Simon or the Portuguese police.

Chapter Nineteen

She held his hand as the plane banked steeply to come in over the harbour at Faro. It took an hour to go through the formalities of filling in and clearing the immigration forms, and while they waited they had bought a local guide book.

The telephone book gave an Albufeira number for Trommer's farm. But the address was Finca da Luz, Tounes, near Albufeira.

They hired a Cortina for a month and paid in advance. The woman recommended some self-catering villas at Golden Beach and got the manager on the telephone for them. They booked adjoining villas.

As they turned out of the airport on to the Portimão road rain lashed down so that the wipers would barely clean the windscreen, drumming on the roof of the car so that talking was impossible.

At the turn-off to Vilamoura the storm abated and as they turned at the signpost that said Praia da Oura the skies were blue again. They drove slowly down the pot-holed roads past the huddles of pink and white houses that flanked the orchards of oranges and lemons. The earth smelled lush from the rain and wisps of steam rose from the pools on the road.

At the cross-roads to Golden Beach he hesitated and turned left, and half a mile further they were at the brow of a hill and the sea lay sparkling before them.

Wallace parked the car half-way down the hill at the reception area for the villas, and a few minutes later they were shown to their adjoining villas.

They unpacked in the first villa and then sat on the balcony looking out to sea. Half an hour later they walked down to the beach. There were heavy storm clouds out to sea but the almost empty beach was bathed in sunshine. They walked hand in hand but in silence, both aware that the beach, the sun and the sea were not why they were there.

The next morning they spent an hour at the supermarket at the cross-roads and then took the short road where the sign pointed to Albufeira. They were able to park the car in the square.

They sat at the corner café. The square was busy, the fruit market on one side, tourist shops on the other, and in the centre of the square a pool and a fountain where children played.

When they had finished their coffees they went back to the car. Wallace found it strangely disturbing to be in a country where there were no official maps, and where the unofficial ones were limited to rough scrawls representing only the twisting main coastal road from Faro to Portimão.

Wallace drove round the square and up the hill to the main road. Five kilometres westward was a small sign that said 'Tounes 6 kms'.

The road twisted and turned through arid countryside where small hump-backed bridges straddled the culverts of dried-up streams. Clumps of spiky pines gave way to cork trees on the stony acres each side of the road. They could see the hills in the distance. At the start of the foothills the road forked and the only sign pointed to the right and said merely 'Purgatorio'.

The road to the left was narrower but there were rows and rows of orange and lemon trees heavy with fruit. At intervals there were cases piled high with fruit at the side of the road. Then the road rose steeply for half a mile and at the top was a sign that said 'Tounes'.

They entered a narrow street and bumped along until they came to what seemed to be the main square. There were a few shops, two cafés and a line of parked cars alongside a garage with petrol pumps. He drew in at the end of the line of cars.

As they walked over to the larger of the two cafés Wallace saw a sign. It said '*Correio*'.

'I think that means post-office, let's try there.'

He found the telephone directory and opened it at Trommer's page and pointed to the name as the man peered through his glasses.

The old man nodded and spoke quickly in Portuguese. Wallace shook his head to show that he didn't understand. The old man walked from behind the counter and pointed to an old map on the wall. It was roughly drawn, yellow with age and was marked with coloured circles.

'*Aqui*.' He said, pointing with one hand to the map and the other at the dirty floor.

He traced a line westwards on the map and said 'Finca da Luz.'

His finger was pointing at a road leading westwards out of the town, and about five miles along that road was the outline of a cluster of buildings.

Wallace offered the old man a cigarette from his pack and he took it, nodding his head. '*Obrigado*.'

They sat outside the café with a bottle of red wine. The people seemed incurious, the women all dressed in black making their small purchases at the shops then going on their way. It reminded Wallace of North Africa. A couple of cars passed through in the half hour they sat there and a man with a small ramshackle lorry unloaded bottles of milk at one of the shops.

They drove round the square and then took the road to the west, past the church and past the railway station.

They passed two farms on the right hand side of the road and then a few miles further on they saw the big, painted sign that said 'Finca da Luz. Prop. W. Trommer'. The gates were six or seven feet high with wooden frames along the top that were festooned with barbed wire. A man with a camouflage jacket and a soft Afrika Korps cap stood at the centre of the gates on the inside. A German Shepherd and a Doberman Pinscher barked furiously as they drove past. Wallace took in the layout of the buildings. There were barns and sheds but there was no sign of a farmhouse.

He turned to look at the girl. 'Welcome to Finca da Luz.'

'It's like a fortress.'

'All that barbed wire is new, my love. And the wooden frame at the top of the gates is new. That's a miniature Fort Knox. They're expecting visitors.'

She was silent and subdued.

'Don't worry, sweetie. We had a place like that on "the Farm".'

'What farm.'

'We called the CIA training centre "the Farm". We had mock frontiers, villages for booby trapping, the lot. We'll get in somehow. Or get him out.'

And as he said it the helicopter seemed to rise silently out of the dead ground on their left, and with its rotors flashing in the sun it banked and turned away to the south. Only as it turned did they hear the clatter of its engine.

'And that's how he gets in and out.'

They were both silent with their separate thoughts all the way back to Golden Beach.

They had walked, after dinner, along the beach and as they leaned back against one of the big rocks she said softly, 'I've got to do it, Hank. I've got to do it.'

'OK. But let me do the recce, Anna. Then we'll talk about it. See what the problems are.'

'I don't care what the problems are.'

'Well you should. You saw in Amsterdam what happens if it isn't planned. Even trained CIA men don't just go charging in on white horses. We take time. We want the maximum odds in our favour. This guy is on his own ground. He'll have influence everywhere. *And* he's expecting you.'

'OK. You do the planning. I'll wait. If it doesn't take too long.'

There were two single beds in his villa so they had slept in hers, a double. When finally they slept, her sleep had been fitful until finally she slid quietly out of bed, swung her dressing-gown around her shoulders and pushed the glass door of the balcony to one side so that she could walk out and look over to the sea.

There was a full moon in the cloudless sky and from the beach she heard the drag of the waves on the line of shingle. A few miles out she could see the golden lights of the fishing boats and their reflection in the sea. Everywhere was still, and quiet, and cool. She drew up one of the plastic chairs so that she could sit with her elbows on the low parapet and with her face cupped in her hands, watch the sea. In the distance she could hear the dull boom where the tide threw tons of green water on some recalcitrant rock, seething in anger as it broke and ravaged the caves behind.

She had looked furtively at the photograph while he was taking a shower. And she was ashamed that for once the figures had lost their power. They were the sad faces that so often stand out from the pages of a newspaper. Something had got between them and her. There was too much to think about. On her own she had been able to concentrate, there was her, and Paul, and them. Her targets just names on a letter in a file. And even when she had seen the two of them it had not been so different. Not different at all so far as Jansen was concerned. She could barely remember his face. Stein had not been what she expected, but that no longer disturbed her. Now, suddenly, there was barbed wire and barking dogs. Surely not for her.

Then she felt his warm hand on her shoulder, and in a moment of terrible reflex she pushed it away and stood up.

'What's the matter, sweetheart?'

And the word sweetheart was like a sword in her body. She wasn't anybody's sweetheart. She was Paul Simon's widow and this stranger must be pushed away. There had been no problems until he came.

She looked up at him. 'I'd rather go on alone, Hank. I did better that way. This way there's too much planning. Not enough doing. You can't help it, I know. You're a man, so you think like a man. When I followed my instincts it worked. I'll come over to Texas when I'm through.'

She was aware of his big brown chest as he took a deep breath. Hairy and masculine. Attractive and animal. She looked at his face expecting anger or rebuttal, but it was calm, and the blue eyes looked back at her as if he were reading some sign in her face.

'What would you have done differently, Anna, if you'd been on your own?'

'Maybe I wouldn't be here, Hank. Maybe I'd be in London dealing with Müller. Not making love in a comfortable bed.'

'We could always cut that out for the time being.'

'You've taken me over, Hank. I'm doing what you say, not what I want.'

'No way, honey. I'm just covering. You give the orders.'

'You mean you'll do whatever I say?'

He sighed. 'I guess so.'

'OK. Let's go and deal with Müller.'

'He won't be there.'

'He may be. You just don't know. We'll wait for him.'

'It would be a long wait, honey.'

'You see. Already you're arguing.'

'I'm not arguing, honey. I'm telling you. Why not leave it at that?'

'Why should I, for God's sake?'

'Müller isn't there and he won't be going back.'

'They said he'd be back in two weeks. It's four weeks now.'

'He won't ever be going back, Anna. He's dead.'

Her mouth opened and her eyes searched his face. She whispered. 'Tell me what you know.'

'I killed him, Anna. He was the man up in the woods, watching the villa. He had a rifle. He was there to kill you.'

She put her hand to her head and despite the heat of the night she was shivering.

'How did they trace me?'

'God knows. But they did.'

He put his arms round her and silently led her back to the bedroom. She lay silently alongside him, staring up at the ceiling, shivering as she listened to the sound of the sea. Then she turned to him and whispered. 'Have me, Hank, just have me.'

They slept late the next day and drove into Albufeira about eleven o'clock. The waiter recognized them and, with a smile, brought them coffee and cakes without being asked.

Something seemed to have changed in the girl overnight. It was she who found his hand, and slid her arm through his; and the pleasure on her face made her even more beautiful. There were plenty of admiring glances by passers-by as they sat outside the café. Wallace bought fresh fruit in the market and they walked to the gift shop and bought a two days' old *Daily Mail*.

They swam at Golden Beach before a late lunch, and Wallace went back to Albufeira in the afternoon to fill up with petrol and have the carburettor checked.

When he came back for the car they were filling up a Volkswagen and the young man who was waiting strolled over to him.

'And who's going to win the election?'

'What election?'

The young man laughed. 'I saw you and your wife buy a *Daily Mail* this morning, so I assumed you were English.'

Wallace smiled. 'I'm afraid not. I'm American, but you can't buy the *New York Times* in Albufeira.'

'Is this your first visit?'

'Yes.'

'It's a good place for a holiday. Where are you staying?'

'Just outside town.'

'Ah well,' the young man said. 'Have a good time.'

As he got to the cross-roads where the track led right to Golden Beach, Wallace stopped at the supermarket to buy milk and he saw the Volkswagen jolt past towards the main Faro road.

Before dinner that evening they drove again to Tounes and past the Finca da Luz. There were two men this time. One sitting smoking on an upturned orange box and the other watching from behind the wire-lattice gates. There were no dogs in sight, but both men had sub-machine guns slung over their shoulders. As they passed through the square at Tounes, the helicopter came in low over the village. It had Portuguese civil markings and he memorized the number painted on the side of the fuselage.

As they drove back down to the Faro road she said, 'You do the planning, Hank. And I'm grateful for what you've done. I was a stupid bitch.'

'Don't worry, kid. It'll get done, I promise you.'

Wallace drove in alone to Faro and used a telephone in the Hotel Eva to make a long call to Stanton Falls.

He was just heading down the hill towards the car park at Golden Beach when he stopped the car and reached over on to the back seat for his binoculars. The Volkswagen was a hundred yards down the hill, parked alongside the hotel that faced the beach. It seemed to be unoccupied and he walked down to the villa.

From the balcony he watched the car through the glasses for an hour. And it was only when he put down the glasses to pull up one of the chairs to the balcony that he saw the glint from way over the cliff-top on the right. He handed the binoculars to the girl and told her to keep watching the Volkswagen.

To the rear of the villa complex was the park for residents' cars, and a few yards beyond that the ground went down almost sheer to an abandoned gravel and sand quarry. Nasturtiums, wild plantain and celandine grew on the steep sides and at the bottom were the barely visible tracks where vehicles had once carried away the tons of sand and gravel. He walked round the top of the quarry until he found where the spring rains had carved a way down the cliff side. He went down slowly and carefully, sometimes sliding helplessly until his heels could dig into the clay.

At the bottom he walked across to the far side, two hundred yards away. It took him fifteen minutes to claw his way up the opposite cliff face, kicking toe-holes in its surface as he clung to trailing roots. At the top he crouched low as he tried to find his bearings. He looked back towards the sun and then split the angle and crawled forward. The reflections from the binoculars had been bright and circular. The ground began to slope and then he saw him. Legs bent, his elbows resting on his knees as he peered through the glasses. It was the man from the Volkswagen.

Slowly and silently he backed away, towards the quarry. At the villa he entered quietly; and standing in the shade of the room he said, 'Don't turn round suddenly, Anna. Just put down the glasses and come inside.'

She lowered the binoculars, placed them on one of the plastic chairs and walked back into the room.

'What is it, Hank? What's going on?'

'There's a young guy been following us around. He spoke to me in Albufeira the other day, and I've seen his car in various places where we've been. Always just out of sight. But he's watching us, that's for sure.'

An hour later, when Wallace checked again, the Volkswagen had gone.

He sat reading the guide book as the girl prepared them a meal, and after they had eaten he drove alone to the Marina at Vilamoura.

An hour later he had paid in advance the two weeks' hire on a Grand Banks 34 footer complete with mooring. He bought food for the galley and had her topped up with diesel. The boat was called the 'Agua Azul' and was registered at Lisbon. The diplomat owner was in Brazil for two years. He locked the cabin and the engine panel, and drove back to Golden Beach.

He said nothing about the boat to the girl.

Chapter Twenty

The next day Wallace hired a second car, a green Mini, and after it had been delivered to the villa he drove it into Albufeira and cashed traveller's cheques at the bank. He watched inside the bank as the girl followed his instructions and drew up at the petrol pumps on the other side of the square. The Volkswagen cruised slowly by and turned towards the cinema. He saw the man walk back to the square and stand, half-hidden by one of the palms, watching the girl. When she drove round the square towards him the man turned casually to look in a shop window. And as her car passed him the man hurried back to the Volkswagen.

Wallace kept a long way behind the Volkswagen and watched it trail the girl to the crossroads and then follow her down the bumpy hill-road to the villas. By the time he got there the Volkswagen was parked down by the beach store.

Wallace spent the afternoon assembling and oiling the PPK. He loaded the chamber carefully.

They strolled down to the beach restaurant, the Borda d'Agua, and lingered over their meal. It was dark by the time they walked back up to the villa. She listened carefully as he told her what to do.

'You go up to the crossroads by the supermarket. You turn right where the sign says Faro. You go on for 6.5 kilometres on the clock and you'll see a sign for Vilamoura. If he's there he'll be about half a kilometre behind you. He'll have his lights on. Don't do more than 40 kpm because I'll be driving with only the moonlight. When I flash my headlights you put your foot down and follow the signs to the marina. Look for mooring 135D on the far side. The boat's named "Agua Azul". Here are the keys. Go on board.

There's a light switch on the right-hand side inside the saloon. Just wait for me, no matter how long I take. OK?'

'OK.'

She kissed him. 'Take care, Hank.'

Despite the full moon and the two sets of car lights ahead of him he had difficulty in keeping the Volkswagen in sight. On the deserted road to Vilamoura he waited until they were past the government agricultural research station and then accelerated, flashing his headlights twice before he crowded the Volkswagen off the road on to the rough edge of the ditch. He cut off the engine and walked over to the other car.

The man was just getting out, staggering slightly as he tried to keep his balance on the uneven ground. Without speaking, Wallace wrenched the man's jacket off his shoulders so that his arms were pinioned.

'Why have you been following that car?'

The man seemed not unduly alarmed as he raised his eyebrows. 'I have my reasons, Mr Wallace.'

'How do you know my name?'

'That's my business.'

Wallace's hand thrust into the young man's hair and wrenched his head backwards.

'Who are you?'

The man shook his head, unable to speak, his eyes screwed up in pain. Wallace released his head.

'Who are you?'

'I'm a policeman, Mr Wallace. I'm investigating the murder in Amsterdam of a Herr Stein. I believe that your lady companion is involved. You may be too.'

'What evidence have you got?'

The young man laughed, and Wallace's fist crashed into his face. He looked back at Wallace with one eye closed, blood seeping from his nose.

'Your violence won't ...' Wallace crashed him back against the tilted side of the Volkswagen.

'What evidence have you got?'

'You bastard.'

And Wallace saw the hand trying to reach inside his jacket. His hand got there first and wrenched the gun from its holster and slid it into his pocket. It was a snub-nosed Smith & Wesson.

'What's your name?'

'Detective de Vries, Royal Netherlands Police Force. And this attack will be part of the evidence I give to the Portuguese Police when I ask for your arrest.'

'How did you trace the girl?'

The young man hesitated for a moment. 'She paid her hotel by American Express. I traced her from that.'

'Where's your warrant?'

'That will come with the application for extradition.'

'Do you really believe she could have committed a murder?'

'After this? I'm damn sure she could. You could too.'

Wallace reached across his chest under his jacket. With his hand still covered he said, 'Are you religious, de Vries?'

'I'm a Roman Catholic, if that's what you mean.'

Wallace nodded. 'Do you want to say a prayer?'

He saw the disbelief and horror on the young man's face. 'Oh no,' he whispered. 'You couldn't do that.'

Wallace pressed the PPK to the man's chest.

'Say it now if it matters.'

'In nomine Patris, filio . . .' And then he screamed, again and again, like an animal; and Wallace pulled the trigger. Twice.

It took him twenty minutes to cram the body into the back of the Mini and drive to the marina.

There were very few boats with lights, and he drove carefully round the feeder-road to the far side of the marina. The lights were on in the boat. The girl was sitting at the saloon table and there was a glass of wine poured out for him. Her own glass was empty. She looked anxiously at his face.

'What happened, Hank? Who was he?'

He held up his hand. 'Don't ask, Anna. It's best you don't know.'

'Tell me what you said to him.'

He shook his head and she saw how drawn his face was.

'Are we going to sleep here on the boat?'

'I'm taking her out to sea first.'

'Tonight?'

'Yes.'

'But why, you look exhausted?'

'I want you to go in the for'ard cabin, and stay there until I tell you to come out.'

'Now?'

'Yes.'

She kissed him and went into the cabin and closed the door.

He sweated with the effort as he manoeuvred the body out of the mini. Rigor was beginning to set in and he looked around the marina as he knelt beside the car. There was nobody about. The last lights had already gone out on the other boats.

He lifted the body and, staggering to his feet, held it across his shoulder in a rough fireman's lift.

On the wheelhouse deck, it lay awkwardly, the legs bent obscenely, and he covered it with a black tarpaulin. Mechanically he warmed the engines, and when they smoked he turned on the ignition and they thumped into life.

He called the harbour master on Channel 16.

'Agua Azul, harbour master. I am leaving for a short run, I expect to return inside two hours. One passenger on board.'

'OK, Agua Azul. Caution, fishing boats off Quarteira, Albufeira and Vale de Lobos. Some without lights in area four kilometres off-shore. Pleasant trip. Use middle channel out and in. Tide nearing full ebb this moment.'

'Thank you, out.'

He cast off the springs and the stern warp and put the starboard engine to 1000 revs. As her head came round he switched on the navigation lights and the main beam. She bucked slightly as he cast off the stern warp and then she was heading for the channel and he put both engines into ahead.

There was a slight swell as they went over the bar and then a longer swell as the tower light gradually faded astern. The lights of the fishing boats were well away from them and he kept to the course as they thumped their way out to sea. He leaned across from the wheel and switched on the Seafarer. It showed seventy fathoms, and he put the engines into neutral. After a few seconds the surface wind was turning her head and she was taking the sea on her beam. He tried to set her on a circular course but she wouldn't take it. She would lose way and roll heavily. There was no way he could leave the wheel.

Eventually, he opened the saloon doors, hooking one back as he called out to the girl.

She came out quickly and stood at the foot of the companion-way steps.

'I'm going to need your help, Anna. Come up here.'

When she stood beside him he put her hands on the wheel.

'I've got to have her making a big circle. Just hold the wheel like this. Don't let it get away from you.'

'OK.'

He pulled out the big Danforth anchor from the locker and payed out about twenty feet of terylene rope. Pushing back the edge of the tarpaulin he lashed the rope to one stiff leg. Then he pulled off the tarpaulin and hauled the body so that it sprawled on the rope locker.

Then he heard the girl scream. He turned quickly and saw that she was staring at the corpse, her hands to her face in horror and the boat rocking madly before he steadied the wheel.

She turned to him, her face distorted in her distress.

'That's Jan de Vries, Hank, how did he get here? Oh my God, what's happened?'

'Who is he?'

'He was a Dutchman I met in Amsterdam.'

178

'He was the man who was tailing you. The man in the Volkswagen. He's a Dutch cop. He was going to apply for your arrest for the murder of Stein. Mine too. There was no choice, Anna.'

Her body was rigid as she held on to the saloon door, her head back, the tendons in her neck taut, shaking her head violently as if it could take away the vision of de Vries' dead body.

'He was a nice man, Hank, he played the violin.'

Wallace tried to control his mounting anger.

'Come and hold the wheel, Anna. Just for another few moments.' She turned like an automaton, sighing as he put her hands on the wheel.

Stumbling over to de Vries' body he lifted it clumsily, taking the anchor in his free hand and then heaved both body and anchor over the side of the boat. He saw the body lie on the water for a moment, turn face downwards and then plunge beneath the waves as the weight of the anchor dragged the body plummeting downwards.

He took the wheel, almost having to force the girl's hands from the leather grip. He set the boat's head into the waves and waited until the compass settled. With his eyes closed he tried to calculate the reciprocal of their course. Then he turned her with both engines in an angry thrashing wash and headed back for the marina. Almost an hour later he saw the tower light a mile off his course on the starboard beam.

Twenty minutes later they tied up at the mooring and he switched off the engines. The sudden silence set his ears ringing as he looked for the girl. She was lying on one of the for'ard bunks, asleep, her mouth agape and with vomit clinging to her clothes. As she slept, breathing stertorously, he gently cleaned her face and then her clothes. He closed the cabin door and threw two of the foam seats on the saloon floor, lay down, and was soon asleep, utterly exhausted.

179

The next day was overcast and grey. They spoke very little as they washed and drank coffee. Finally the girl said, 'It's crazy, Hank, but I want to make love.'

He looked at her across the small saloon table.

'That's not crazy, sweetheart. It's normal.'

'How is it normal, Hank?'

'After the Germans bombed Guernica in the Spanish Civil war the survivors went into the fields and made love. After battles soldiers want women. After plane crashes survivors, strangers, have had sex. It's a primitive thing. It celebrates escape and I suppose it ensures the survival of the species.'

'Did you feel like that after doing CIA things?'

'Yes.'

'You made love to strange girls?'

'Sometimes. Not always.'

'Why not always?'

'It wasn't always possible.'

'Do you want me now?'

'You know I do.'

'Can you draw the curtains?'

He glanced round the saloon.

'They are drawn.'

He watched as she undressed, her shoulders and belly tanned from being in the sun while she had been practising the karate moves, her full breasts white and trembling and the black fleece between her long legs. He took her with urgent lust, having her again and again as if he were never going to have a girl again in his life. And she responded eagerly, her body clinging to his, her eyes closed as she begged him not to stop.

When they were finally still she looked at him and said:

'I wish we were married this minute, Hank. I wish it so much.'

He kissed her gently. 'We can wait, my love. It won't be long.'

'You understand don't you, Hank?'

'Understand what?'

'I'll have paid my debt, and we can start a new life.'

'You don't need to forget Paul for me, sweetie. If you loved him I'm sure I would have liked him too.'

She looked up at him. 'Is it too soon to do it again?'

He smiled. 'No.'

From the marina clubhouse he called the Lisbon number again. It was good to hear an American accent.

'The first bit's not on, Hank. I didn't think it would be. But I've fixed the second thing. You're a member as of yesterday.'

'There's no deal I could do on the photograph?'

'No way, Hank. The satellites do cover the area you mentioned but there isn't a cat in hell's chance of getting hold of one.'

'Not even an old one, an out-of-date one?'

'Not a chance.'

'The club membership gives me a licence?'

'Automatically, no problem.'

'Are there any competitions coming up?'

'I don't know. You'll have to check with the club.'

They drove across to Golden Beach, collected their things and paid the bill. Wallace implied that they were leaving for Faro airport immediately.

Back at the marina they stowed away their stuff and the girl got them a meal.

'I'm going to Lisbon tomorrow, Anna. I'll be back in the evening. Maybe you could meet me in at the airport.'

'Of course. Maybe I'll stay in Faro all day.'

'Book a room for us at the big hotel. I think it's called the Eva. We'll stay there for the night.'

It was ten o'clock when the Lisbon plane landed and as she stood watching she saw him in the first group of passengers walking across the tarmac. As the ground steward opened the door to the reception area a policeman stopped Wallace and it was only then she saw the gun-case over his shoulder, the canvas and leather new, a label tied to one of the straps.

She saw Wallace pull an envelope from his jacket pocket and hand it over. The officer opened the papers inside and read them carefully. When he had handed them back he pointed at the case and Wallace undid the straps. He lifted out one rifle, and then to her surprise another. The officer looked at them and nodded and waved Wallace on through the open door.

As he came through the exit gate he was smiling as he took her arm.

'Which car did you bring?'

'The big one.'

'Good.'

He shoved the gun-case and a canvas bag in the boot of the Cortina and locked it. Checking it twice.

In her room he seemed elated as he sat on the bed looking at her.

'I had an inspiration when I was in Lisbon. I went along to the Land Registry and the Agricultural Registry. I've got photocopies of the whole area of Trommer's place. Not drawn too well and not all that accurate to a metre or two, but good enough.'

'Do they help?'

'There's a way in. A stream that runs across the whole estate. They're not allowed to block it off. I'll do a recce tomorrow.'

'Why the two guns?'

'One for you and one for me.'

'I want to do it myself, Hank.'

182

'OK.'

She didn't know him well enough to notice the muscles at his jaw, and if she *had* noticed she would probably not have recognized that they were caused by anger and frustration kept too long under control.

He had joined her in something with which he entirely disagreed. That he saw as at best, mis-directed love. And at worst, an eye-for-an-eye revenge that was as crude and amoral as the deed that had killed her husband and child.

He was involved in the beginning because he loved her and wanted to protect her, but now it was no longer mere involvement. And it wasn't solely because he loved her any-more. He was doing things now to protect them both. It irked him, her insistence that she completed her plan. Three of the ODESSA men responsible were already dead. What was the magic in killing the fourth? It smacked of a Ger-manic thoroughness that had nothing to do with love, and little enough of humanity. What if the list was incorrect or spurious? Were the Document Centre always so accurate? And it irked him that she wouldn't leave it to him. She was swimming in water far too deep for her. Almost too deep for him. And in his turn he felt disloyal to her for even mentally criticizing her when she was now so obviously committed to him. He must save what he could out of the shambles for both of them.

It was late afternoon when he parked the Mini under the trees. He lifted out the binoculars and then started the scramble across the hill. When he got to the stream he was surprised to find it running strongly. He had half expected nothing more than a trickle, or even a dried up pathway. He put in his hand and the water was icy cold despite the strong sun. It probably came from high up in the mountains to the west.

He went back, away from the stream, it was too much of a landmark. He made for a clump of pines and lay in their shade. Far away he could hear dogs barking and then the

183

groaning engine of an overloaded truck. They were probably opening the gates for a truck to go out.

Then suddenly he heard voices and he turned his head to look in their direction. He leaned up on his elbows to look further and saw them at least half a mile away. A concrete circle had been laid in the centre of a small plateau on the sloping ground and the rotors of the helicopter were slowly turning, and then a burst of noise as the engine fired. There were five men that he could see. The pilot with a clipboard in his hand, was talking to a stocky man who stood listening and nodding, with his hands on his hips. He wore black riding breeches and black riding boots and he looked every inch an SS man. His grey hair was crew-cut and he was the only man there who was old enough to be Trommer. As he watched, the pilot clambered into the helicopter and swung the door to.

For a moment or two the helicopter seemed to be straining to take off, its landing wheels stretching tentatively, and then it was up, rising vertically, its tail slowly swinging, banking as it circled to the south.

Then he saw the man pointing and the others were putting lamps at the cross-points of the landing pad. It looked as if the chopper was going to come back after dark.

An hour later it was almost dark and he was picking up his binoculars to move when he saw the torches less than a hundred yards away. There were two men, and they were talking together as they walked towards him, following the bank of the stream. Every few yards they stopped and fanned their torches into the darkness. When they were almost dead ahead they stopped, and one walked slowly down towards the clump of pines. He called back something in Portuguese to the other man who laughed. As the torch played across the upper branches of the trees, Wallace buried his head in the dry grass. The man stood still, whistling softly through his teeth, and then Wallace heard him turn and slowly walk away. He lifted his head and looked out cautiously. The two of them were going on their way.

184

It took him almost an hour to find even low cover that was near to the landing pad and a thin heat mist was rising from the ground. It was nearly midnight when the men came out to light the lamps. And fifteen minutes later he could hear the clatter of the helicopter.

The SS type was giving out orders and then Wallace heard what he had been waiting for. Someone said '*Si Sinhor Trommer*' and Trommer nodded his head in acknowledgment. If he had had the rifle with him he could have shot him clean and easy. But he wouldn't have got away.

As the chopper came back in he took advantage of the noise and activity to stumble back through the dry grass to the clump of pines and then up the slope and along the stream. He walked quietly down the road towards where he had parked the car.

He saw the reflection of moonlight on the Mini's windscreen and smelt the smoke of a cigarette as he got to the car. For a moment he hesitated. Somebody had been checking the car. Then he got in the car and started the engine. If they had been watching his car they were probably going to tail him. Instead of turning right, down the hill to the Faro road, he turned left, up the hill, and another right turn took him on to the road past the gates of the Finca da Luz. He went past at normal speed and saw two guards dressed in camouflage kit outside the gates, which were half open. Inside the gates a man in dark clothes was talking into a portable radio, its aerial glinting in the moonlight.

He stopped the car in the square at Tounes. He had seen a sign when they were up there that said *Pensão*. He walked round the moonlit square. It was in the far corner and there was a faint light from one of the downstairs windows.

He rang the bell and waited. There were shufflings in the hallway and an old man opened the door, his hand curved to his ear.

Wallace held out a 1,000 escudos note and put his head sideways on his hand, hoping the old man would understand.

The old man nodded. *'Um quarto para esta noite'* he said, reaching for the note. He stood aside and Wallace walked in. He followed the old man slowly up the stairs and on the second landing the old man unlocked a door and gave him the key.

It was quite a big room. Clean, with an old-fashioned bed and a big wardrobe. It was all he needed.

He took off his shoes and lay back on the bed. Far away he heard a telephone ringing, and then he was asleep.

He seemed to have slept for a long time before he heard the footsteps on the stairs, but he was half awake when the door crashed open and someone flashed a torch on his face.

As his eyes became accustomed to the light from the landing he saw that there were two men standing at the open door. One of them was Trommer.

The telephone that he had heard ringing as he went off to sleep must have been one of Trommer's men checking in the village when they lost track of the Mini.

Wallace reached out to the old-fashioned bedside lamp and switched it on.

Trommer stood just inside the door, still in his semi-SS outfit, his hands aggressively on his hips, his legs astride. His face was like a battered stone carving. Flattened nose, prognathous jaw and a crumpled ear. He walked forward.

'You are English, yes?' he said.

'Who are you?'

'Is no matter. You are English?'

'Get out of my room.'

Trommer's eyes narrowed. 'This gentleman is from police. You will answer his questions.'

The other man wore denim trousers, a plaid shirt and well worn shoes. Trommer signalled him to come forward and reluctantly he stood alongside Trommer. He spoke rapidly in Portuguese and Wallace shrugged and opened his arms, shaking his head to indicate that he couldn't understand.

Trommer said, 'He asks why you were trespassing on my estate.'

186

Wallace's blue eyes looked at Trommer coldly.

'Are you a policeman?'

'No. I am the owner of the estate.'

Wallace stood up, his eyes still on Trommer's face.

'If you are not police, then get the hell out of my room.'

'I am ...'

'I don't give a damn who you are,' Wallace roared. 'I'll give you thirty seconds to get out or I'll put you out myself.'

Trommer turned and spoke to the policeman in Portuguese ignoring Wallace and his threat. He only realized that the threat was real as Wallace's arm went round his bull neck. The German's body was hard and solid and his big paw came up to wrench at Wallace's arm. His fingers were thick and strong, and as Trommer braced himself to put Wallace over his shoulder, Wallace's knuckle went up behind Trommer's ear, twisting and turning until the German screamed with pain. Even in pain he struggled, and Wallace slid the knuckle up to the final pressure point and the German's hand released his arm as his stocky body staggered and fell.

As Wallace and the policeman looked down at Trommer a quiet voice said in English, 'Perhaps I can help you.'

A tall slim man stood bare-footed, wearing an old-fashioned flannel dressing-gown. A lock of his sparse fair hair hung over one eye. He looked at Wallace. 'My name is Mathews. I'm a lecturer on plant hybrids, visiting institutions here. I live in Tounes most of the year. What's the problem?'

'This man,' he said pointing at Trommer, 'burst into my room demanding to know who I was. He says this man is a policeman. I told the man to get out and he didn't. We struggled. He's not badly hurt, but he'll be unconscious for about an hour.'

Mathews spoke to the policeman who replied at length.

'He's the village policeman. Not very bright, I'm afraid. Our friend on the floor is a very important local farmer. A German named Trommer. He probably pays the policeman a small stipend to turn a blind eye on occasions or generally do what he's told. Trommer said your car was parked on his land.'

'It was parked just off a public road. If it had been parked in his front garden that would be no excuse for bursting into my room in the middle of the night.'

Mathews nodded and talked some more with the policeman. When he turned back to Wallace he said, 'It seems Trommer has received some anonymous threat to his life and he's very touchy about strangers. I've said that you and I will go to the police station tomorrow morning. Is that agreeable to you?'

'What are they charging me with?'

'Nothing. It's a face-saving device. He'll take your name and address and that will be it. Because of Trommer a report will go in to Faro and that will be that. Trommer's important and influential, but you're right, he made a mistake bursting in here tonight. The Faro police won't like that. He must be pretty windy to have gone to these lengths.'

'Well, thanks for your help.'

'You're welcome, my friend. I'll tell the policeman to let Trommer's minions take him away.'

He spoke to the policeman who nodded and walked on to the landing and called down.

It took two of Trommer's men and the policeman to get the heavy body down the stairs.

The next morning Wallace paid the old man another week's rent before leaving with Mathews.

'Let's not rush. We'll have a coffee first, Mr Wallace. We've got a front to keep up too with our Nato Allies.'

At the one-roomed police-station, Mathews did the interpreting. Wallace showed his passport and gave the pension as his local address.

Mathews invited him for another drink and they sat in the sunshine, chatting.

'Trommer's a pretty good horticulturalist, you know.

188

Modern strains, modern methods and plenty of capital.'

'What does he grow?'

'Oranges, lemons, satsumas, all the citrus fruits. Four hundred acres of vines and thirty thousand head of poultry. Layers and broilers.'

'Where did the money come from?'

'God knows. These refugee Germans were all well off. There's some local money in the enterprise, and I'd guess there's a bit of political money in there too. He had more influence in Salazar's day, before the revolution. But even when the revolution was on they didn't touch Trommer's place.'

'Was he well in with the PIDE boys?'

'How do you know about them?'

Wallace shrugged. 'There were always bits in the newspapers about them.'

'His helicopter pilot is an ex-PIDE man.'

'Why does Trommer need a chopper?'

'It's partly status symbol and partly necessity. They move the day's cash and cheques to the bank in Faro every night. It does a bit of field spraying and he goes to Lisbon quite often. He can afford it anyway.'

'Is he liked locally?'

'Oh no. The locals hate him. He treats them like slaves. They see him as a left-over piece of the old regime. He's tolerated officially, but no more.'

'Is this just because he's rich?'

'God no. There are half a dozen men between here and Faro richer than Trommer. He's just an out and out bastard. He sees himself as a local baron, outside the law and monarch of all he surveys. You experienced it yourself last night. The Portuguese don't like that sort of behaviour. They're law-abiding and non-violent. The Trommers of this world embarrass them. Another drink?'

'No thanks. How about you?'

'I must be getting on my way. I'll see you at the *pension* I expect.'

Wallace sat there for a few moments collecting his thoughts. He had kept away from the girl and the boat, and apart from his name they had no idea who he was. He knew now how to get onto the estate, and he now knew a lot about Trommer and it looked as if the locals and the police might not be all that zealous in hunting down somebody who gave Trommer his final come-uppance.

He checked in the Mini at the hire firm and hired another white Cortina. There had been no indication that he was being followed as he took a circuitous route back to Vila-moura.

The girl, white-faced and tense, was obviously relieved to see him back, and he told her what had happened.

'We'll have to do it in the next two days, Anna. There are too many people on the look out for us. De Vries probably had to report every day. Because of Trommer, the police are aware of me. Sooner or later they'll close in on us.'

'How can we do it, Hank?'

He took a deep breath, closing his eyes for a moment before he looked at her face. 'It's much easier for me to do it alone, Anna, it really is.'

He sighed as she shook her head.

'I want to do it, Hank, I want to finish what I started. I need to. It's so that I ... we ... can start afresh.'

He knew it was futile to argue and he said quietly, 'You get us something to eat and I'll get the boat ready.'

'Where are we going?'

'Just out to sea. I want to show you how to use the rifle.'

Wallace cleared with the harbour-master as he headed for the main channel. The sea was calm and only a small off-shore breeze ruffled its surface. There were tankers and merchant ships on the horizon, but even when they were ten miles off-shore they seemed no nearer. The sea lane was a further five miles out. They could no longer see the shore-line.

190

The only remaining anchor was an old-fashioned Fisherman's anchor and Wallace checked the buckle and the chain. There were about forty fathoms of rope and the Seafarer showed twenty-five under them. Wallace slackened the line to the winch and cranked a few fathoms around the cylinder. Dragging the heavy weight to the break in the pulpit, he lifted it and heaved it into the sea.

Slowly the boat swung in the tide, the fluke bit in the seabed, dragged for a few feet and then bit again.

They ate while he checked the two rifles and he tossed out a white plastic fender on a long nylon line. When it was about 75 yards away he wrapped the end round a chromium cleat on the foredeck.

He took out the saloon seat covers for her to lie on and after checking the setting on the micrometer sights he gave her the rifle. For an hour he taught her how to load and sight, fire and check and reload.

He gave her six shots at the plastic fender and she nicked it with the last shot. At the end of another hour she could hit it somewhere with every shot. She was delighted with her new skill. But as he clambered to his feet he knew how useless it was. It was a moving erratic target, admittedly, and it was roughly the size of a man's head, but reality was not going to be lying on cushions, and there would only be one shot.

She turned on her side to look at him, smiling. 'Are you pleased with me, Hank?'

He crouched down with bent knees beside her.

'You did fine, sweetheart. Really fine.'

He saw the look in her eyes and he stretched out alongside her and her arms went round him as he pushed up her skirt.

It was early evening when he took out the Cortina. He kept well away from Tounes and the Finca da Luz, but near enough to watch through the binoculars the evening take-off of the helicopter. Take off time was 9.12 p.m. local time. It

191

was one of Aerospatiale's little Alouettes. He wasn't sure
which variation, but it was at least twelve years old.

It came back and landed at 11.45, as he sat watching in the
darkness trying to sort out his thoughts. There were too
many strands, Tom and the store, Anna, the Dutch police,
his physical desire, the idea of a real home, her dead husband and the problem of Trommer. And all the sub-strands
of wishes and prejudices, self-preservation and love. You
couldn't feed them into two sides of a pair of scales and see
which side they came down. How did you balance love
against second-hand murder? How did you balance her husband's death against ODESSA men? Maybe the bastards
should just have been left to rot. And then he had the image
of Trommer. Arrogant and brutal. *He* would have lost no
sleep over the murder of Paul Simon. And how do you
weigh the scales between the girl's certain arrest and the
killing of a man she described as 'nice' because he played the
violin. Didn't Streicher or Himmler or one of the top Nazis
play the violin?

He shivered in silence as a night breeze swept across the
hill. What would Tom think if he married again? He had
liked Anna but she wasn't a potential step-mother then. He
shook his head as if that might get him off the treadmill.
There must be wise men somewhere, he thought, who you
could give these problems to for perfect solutions. Sooth-
sayers, oracles, priests; but nowadays it was headshrinkers
and those little blue capsules.

When he had spoken to Tom and his father on the
telephone they sounded so sane, so normal; and they took it
for granted that at long last he had collected his battered
feelings from the divorce and was sensibly taking time out.
He was the one they all looked to to keep their lives on an
even keel. He had been conscious in the unhappy months
leading to the inevitable divorce, of people watching him,
learning lessons, taking note of how a man should behave
when a wife openly and publicly flaunts her infidelity. When

it had first started he had ignored the advice that was show-
ered on him, to abandon her to her fate. Popular opinion
said she was heading inexorably for the gutter, and outsiders
saw that as reason enough to cut the bond that kept them
together. But that wasn't his way. Although he didn't understand the compulsion itself, he understood its source and
reasons. She wasn't doing it to him. She wasn't, consciously,
doing it to herself. She was showing all those who hadn't
cared for her when she was a child, that others cared for her,
that others found her desirable. The fact that those old
enemies were indifferent rather than hostile, and were now
hundreds of miles away was not in her knowledge. Neigh-
bours, friends, wondered aloud why her fancy men always
took her to Akron. Hank Wallace knew, but never said. The
orphanage had been at Akron. Sympathy for an oft-
cuckolded man soon wears thin. Tolerance and forbearance
can be construed as indifference, and it's easier to fall back
on the old music-hall jokes. She always relied on him to be
there when she came back. But there came a time when she
sensed that one day the door could be closed. It was then
that she had started taking the boy. She reasoned that he
would always be her insurance. The key that opened the
door. It was only at that point that he had cut the rope and
set her adrift.

He stood up slowly, and even as he stood he knew what he
had to do. Thinking didn't solve these sort of problems.
Actions produced the solutions. The right actions, for the
right reasons, had an inevitability of outcome. Somewhere
in the next twenty-four hours there would be some touchstone, some indicator about their lives from what he had to
do to save the girl from herself.

Without having solved his problem he had sorted out the
strands from each other and he drove back to the marina
with his mind clear and alert; and in those few kilometres he
went over the details of his plans for the next day.

She was waiting for him; sitting in the wheelhouse in a

white cotton nightgown, her long black hair tied with a red ribbon. With her knees bent and her head resting on her knees she looked incredibly young and innocent.

'Did you do whatever you wanted to do?'

'Yes.'

'I went for a walk while you were away. I bought you something.'

He smiled. 'What is it?'

She pointed to the saloon. 'It's on the table.'

He walked down the short companionway and looked across at the table. There was a thin blue and grey vase of local pottery and in its narrow neck a long stemmed red rose.

He turned to look back at her, and she said, 'I love you, Hank.'

She saw the sparkle of tears in his eyes and held out her arms to him.

Chapter Twenty-Two

Wallace sketched out the buildings and boundaries of the Finca da Luz and marked in the roads up to Tounes, the road past the gates and the road to the west that led down to the main Faro road. He went over what she had to do again and again.

'Up the east road to Tounes — this one here — to arrive about one o'clock. Turn left the way we always do on to the road past Trommer's place. Drive past normally — not slowly, not fast — don't turn your head but check what is going on. Keep going until you see my Cortina parked just this side of the turn of the west road. Have you got that?'

'Yes, Hank. What if anything happens?'

'Like what?'

'I don't know.'

'If you're in any doubt at all about what you should do you just drive on down the Faro road and come back here to the boat.'

'And when I get to your car?'

'Either I'll be there or there will be a message for you on the driver's seat. Do whatever the message says. If you get stopped by the police or anybody, you are just driving around because of insomnia. OK?'

'OK.'

'I've got some things to do in Faro. How about I take you to the Eva. You stay there while I do my jobs and then we'll eat. This afternoon we'll take the boat out.'

'What are we going to do on the boat?'

'Absolutely nothing.'

It took him an hour to find where he could hire a cycle. He strapped it to the roof-rack and then drove to the airport.

He sat for a long time at a table in the departure café, writing and stopping, then writing again. He sealed the two envelopes and slid them in his jacket pocket. Back at the Cortina he slid the envelopes under the mat in the boot.

They ate a leisurely lunch and for the first time in weeks Wallace felt relaxed. He knew what had to be done; it was not knowing that always drained his spirit.

They cleared with the marina harbour-master by early afternoon and cruised westwards anchoring off Albufeira. Wallace put out the foam cushions and seats on the foredeck and fixed up the striped awning from the coach-house roof.

They made love, and then he slept, and she watched him while he was sleeping. His body was a deep brown, the muscles on his arms and legs were relaxed and his chest rose and fell softly like a child's. There was a white scar up his right forearm and a star shaped scar on his left side just below his ribs. He seemed a strange man, all of a piece but the pieces were somehow both childlike and adult at the same time. He made love energetically and enthusiastically but without sophistication. Like a young boy rather than an adult. She found it physically satisfying and faintly romantic. But his mind was an adult mind, masculine, primitive and seemingly all-knowing about the ways of the world, how to survive in any environment. Whatever he had been, or done, in the CIA, had not made him outwardly hard or cynical and she knew that she was lucky to have him, both now and for the future. She would find it strange at first in the small Texas town, but they would have a bond between them that few couples ever had. It would be like Pierre and his wife who had the bond of their years in the camps. And there were planes from Texas, so that sometimes they could come back to France. It was odd, she thought, faintly unnatural, that France was home for her, not Germany. She had been virtually unaware of history or the outside world when she lived in Germany. Perhaps it was like that for everyone when they were growing up. They had been taught about the Nazis, and the students at Göttingen had spent

196

hours discussing them. But without involvement, much as if they were discussing the Goths, the Romans or some obscure Polynesian tribe whose obscene customs lent themselves to philosophical discussion.

She leaned over and gently kissed his mouth and her hand slid down between his legs.

They tied up in the marina just after six o'clock and Wallace carefully checked every one of the ten rounds before putting five of each into his shirt pockets. He slid out the bolt and checked the action again and again. Then with the bolt in place and drawn back, slid a round inside and eased the bolt forward and downwards. He checked the movement of the safety catch and left it at 'safety'.

He checked the engine, lights and brakes of both Cortinas and the straps on the cycle, working slowly and thoroughly, despite his mounting tension. Trying to keep his mind solely on what he was doing. There were brief moments when he wondered if what he was intending to do was not stupid or exaggerated. But he kept grimly on with his checking.

At nine o'clock he was ready to go. Standing in front of her he made her go over again the timing and the route.

'Don't start off from here before midnight or you'll have time to waste and it's easy to find yourself too far away to get back in time.'

'OK, Hank,' and, smiling, gave him a mock salute. He kissed her gently and she sat watching him from the wheelhouse as he walked in the fading light to the car.

He parked the Cortina in the square at Tounes, and unstrapped the cycle. He pedalled past the gates of the Finca da Luz without turning his head but from the corner of his eye he saw that there were the usual two men in camouflage kit standing inside the gate. He carried on to the junction of the next road and hid the cycle in a clump of gorse at the junction. It would be easier and quicker to come on foot up the hill rather than riding a cycle.

197

He went on to the estate, well below the bridge over the stream, and made a wide circle in the dead ground about half a mile beyond the helicopter pad. The light was too poor to sight precisely on the centre of the pad. There was good cover where he lay but he wasn't happy about the line of fire. Because of the slope, the trajectory would take the shot only inches above the ground for the first two hundred feet and ground wind and eddies could make the line unreliable.

The outline of the helicopter gradually faded, and far away, up by the stream, he saw the flashing torches as the guards carried out their routine check.

He saw the flare of a match and then the glow of another until there was a light at each end of the points on the pad. The breeze veered and he could hear the voices quite plainly but they were talking in Portuguese.

Trommer talked with the pilot and stood watching as he climbed the metal ladder. Stepping back to the edge of the pad, Trommer signalled to the pilot.

For almost thirty seconds Trommer's face was illuminated like the chiaroscuro of some old master painting, and then with a roar of its engine and the rotors levelling as they picked up speed, the chopper lifted, edging slightly forward to avoid the thermals off the hill-side. Then it swung slowly and headed east for Faro.

Wallace could see the men checking the lights, pumping the pressure pistons and adjusting the flames. Trommer stood in the centre and Wallace lined up the sights on his head and was tempted.

He had planned to wait for the helicopter's return. At the take-off there was always more tension, more awareness. When it landed people would be relaxing, the night's work done and beds and food in the offing.

One man stayed when the others had left, shading his eyes with one hand from the light of the lamps, he looked out into the darkness beyond the light, but Wallace knew that he would see nothing but the blackness. The guards and the

Dobe went over to the man, the dog straining at its leash to reach forward to the friendly hand. They talked for a few minutes and then walked off together.

In the silence after they had gone, Wallace could hear the soft roar of the pressure lamps, despite the distance.

Slowly and carefully he worked his way across the dead ground, up the hill, until he was on the same level as the helicopter pad. He no longer had any cover, but the trajectory was safer. He sighted on the lamps again and again, making minute adjustments to the sight. When he was satisfied he lay the rifle down on the dry grass bolt side up. He backed away a few paces, and then, kneeling, undid his flies and relieved himself.

He crawled back and settled down to wait. He tried to check the time on his watch, but there wasn't enough light. Rolling on to his side he unbuttoned the flap of his right-hand shirt pocket and eased out the long, thin rounds. His thumb touched each tip carefully. He could feel the crosses that he had filed on them and touched each one to his tongue to check their roughness. He knew they had been perfectly done, he had checked them in bright sunlight. It was no more than the pitcher at a ball-game, touching his cap for the third time before throwing the ball. He took the folded Kleenex from his hip pocket and put it alongside the rifle with the rounds lying on it, parallel to each other, their tips all forward.

It was half an hour before he heard the helicopter returning and when he lifted his head he could see it almost two miles away. Its interior was lit, and as he watched, its belly light came on. He pulled the rifle to him and laid his right hand along its stock. Trommer was standing at the edge of the pad, hands on hips, giving orders to his men. The chopper came lower and lower, then circled a couple of times to test the thermals and as he saw it centre on the pad he pulled up the rifle.

He sighted on Trommer's ear, squeezed the trigger, reloaded and lined-up the sights on the helicopter which was about twenty feet from the ground. He fired again. The plexi-glass housing shattered, and the helicopter hung nose down for a second before plunging into the ground, its fuselage lattice crumpled and hanging by one strut. Trommer was on the ground and the men were rushing between his body and the helicopter in panic. Then the petrol ignited, bursting into flames and flowed across the pad to set fire to the grass.

Wallace ran for the stream, stowed the rifle under the bridge and made for the top road. His legs were stiff and heavy from lying still so long. At the top of the hill he turned on to the road that led to Tounes, past the gates at the Finca da Luz.

Before he got to the gates he stumbled further up the hillside and, crouching, went on another hundred yards before he came down again to the road. As he turned and stopped to catch his breath he saw flames thirty feet in the air, outlining the farm buildings and flickering eerily on the tops of the trees. He guessed that the chopper must have refuelled at Faro.

It was ten minutes before he reached the square at Tounes and he hurriedly wiped the sweat from his face and arms as he sat in the Cortina. He drove off, without lights, and minutes later he passed the big gates and headed for the road junction. He left the keys in the ignition and opened the boot. He took out the two envelopes, checked them and put one on the driver's seat.

There were pieces of gorse caught in the wheel spokes of the bicycle and as he free-wheeled down the hill to the main road they chinged and whirred against the forks until they were cut to pieces.

On the main road he checked his watch. It wasn't yet 12.15 and the girl would still be safely at the boat. He ped-alled steadily, taking short cuts across rough ground and walking the cycle past houses where there were lights. He had maybe cut it too fine. It was 12.50 when he got to the boat. He washed hurriedly and threw his stuff quickly into

200

the canvas hold-all. He had ordered the taxi for one-fifteen. Pray God it came on time.

A voice shouted to him from the quayside and he pulled aside a curtain. It was the taxi driver. He waved back and closed the curtain. Then he pulled out the second envelope, hesitated for a moment, and then put it in the centre of the saloon table.

In the taxi he put back his head and closed his eyes. He looked at his watch as the taxi dropped him at the airport buildings. He paid the driver and ran inside and heard the Tannoy.

'This is the last call for passengers for the TAP flight to Lisbon boarding at Gate 9 please.'

Remembering what he had said, she stopped for five minutes just outside Tounes and then threaded her way through the square. She was aware of people, and thought it was strange so late at night when the square was normally empty. Then she was on the west road and saw the flames and a pall of grey smoke as she approached the Finca da Luz.

There were cars with flashing lights and a policeman stepped out and waved her down. She let down the window and he said, 'Cuidado. Houve um desastre.'

'I'm a stranger,' she said slowly in English. He nodded and waved her on.

As she went slowly by she saw fire-engines, an ambulance and police cars. She knew then that he had done it alone.

She drove on until she saw the other white Cortina. Even that distance away the air was thick with smoke and she hurried to the car, opened the door and snatched the envelope from the seat.

Holding it in front of her car's headlights she read what it said.

'GO STRAIGHT TO THE BOAT'.

She stood looking back towards Trommer's place. A whole field seemed to be alight, sparks flying into the air and

201

smoke billowing upwards in clouds. As she watched she realized that it was the end of her journey. The debt had been paid. She felt no elation, no victory, just tiredness, and she shivered as she got back into the car.

She saw his cycle propped against the hand rails as she drove on to the feeder road and she parked alongside the jetty.

The lights were on on the boat.

She called out. 'Hank, I'm back.'

She opened the saloon doors and went slowly down the steps. Something was wrong. She could sense it. Please God he wasn't hurt.

Then she saw the envelope on the saloon table. Alongside the rose in the vase.

She tore it open, hurriedly, untidily, and spread out the two pages of writing.

She read slowly, her mouth silently forming the words.

Dearest Anna,

By the time you read this you will know that I have dealt with T. There was no doubt in my mind that it was far too dangerous for you to tackle. I couldn't face leaving you to walk into all that alone, no more than I could stand by and see young Tom get beaten up.

Despite our circumstances my mind has been mainly on us. I can remember so well that day at Stanton Falls when I saw you smile. I felt a great surge of pleasure because until that moment you had always looked so sad. And now, I wish that I could put the clock back and be wiser for us both.

There is no doubt in my mind that I have been both stupid and weak. Because I love you so much I never found the courage to dissuade you from your plans. I felt that if the choice lay between me and those plans then I should lose. So I went along with it all, and we both know what this has meant. Men who are that besotted are poor partners in a marriage.

Always I found an excuse. If I stuck to my views I should

202

lose you and it wouldn't even stop you. You would be killed, I was sure of that. How could I leave you and let that happen. The reasons I gave you to persuade you not to go on were genuine and real. But always at the back of my mind I realized that it was partly for my sake, our sake, that I put them forward. You seemed to be struggling across a bridge from one life to another. A bridge that wouldn't carry my weight as well as your own. I'm no good at saying what I mean and I'm not all that sure what I do mean.

I understood your motives even though I didn't agree with what you were doing. Most people would feel great compassion for you. I felt love as well. But when I look at it I was really no more than a hired hand. Not because you meant it that way but it just turned out that way. And when it was all over I could claim my payment. You.

In a way I seem stronger, more capable, than you, but in reality I'm not. You were the strong one. If you had had my training you wouldn't have needed me. It was as if your car broke down and I got it going again and drove you back to town. I know you liked me, but I realize that the rest was probably gratitude. And both of us persuaded ourselves that it was more. But if we were married there would be days when one of us looked at the other and wondered what our marriage was built on. And then we should be on very thin ice. There would be too many things we should want to forget.

I told you once that I was sure that people paid for these things but I wasn't sure how. I'm sure how I'm going to pay. I'm paying right now with this letter. I would gladly pay for the two of us.

Sometimes I had pictures in my mind of you in the sunshine in Stanton Falls, and the two of us getting in the car to go to the movies or a meal, and teaching you to ride and fish. But be sure I'll be thinking about you in the villa at Aix and the smell of the mimosa. Think of me sometimes.

I love you.
Hank W.

THE WORLD'S GREATEST THRILLER WRITERS –
NOW AVAILABLE IN GRANADA PAPERBACKS

Len Deighton

Twinkle, Twinkle, Little Spy	£1.25	☐
Yesterday's Spy	£1.25	☐
Spy Story	£1.25	☐
Horse Under Water	95p	☐
Billion Dollar Brain	£1.25	☐
The Ipcress File	£1.25	☐
An Expensive Place to Die	95p	☐
Declarations of War	95p	☐
Bomber	£1.50	☐
The Best of Len Deighton Gift Set	£5.95	☐

Peter Van Greenaway

Doppelganger	60p	☐
The Medusa Touch	85p	☐
Take the War to Washington	75p	☐
Judas!	75p	☐
Suffer! Little Children	95p	☐

Ted Allbeury

Snowball	95p	☐
A Choice of Enemies	95p	☐
Palomino Blonde	95p	☐
The Special Collection	60p	☐
The Only Good German	85p	☐
Moscow Quadrille	75p	☐
The Man with the President's Mind	85p	☐

THE WORLD'S GREATEST THRILLER WRITERS –
NOW AVAILABLE IN GRANADA PAPERBACKS

Robert Ludlum

The Chancellor Manuscript	£1.50 ☐
The Gemini Contenders	£1.25 ☐
The Rhinemann Exchange	£1.25 ☐
The Matlock Paper	£1.25 ☐
The Osterman Weekend	£1.25 ☐
The Scarlatti Inheritance	£1.25 ☐
Ludlum Super-Thrillers Gift Set	£5.95 ☐

Ian Fleming

Dr No	95p ☐
From Russia, with Love	95p ☐
Diamonds are Forever	95p ☐
On Her Majesty's Secret Service	95p ☐
Goldfinger	85p ☐
You Only Live Twice	95p ☐
Live and Let Die	95p ☐
The Man with the Golden Gun	95p ☐
Octopussy	75p ☐
Casino Royale	75p ☐
Thunderball	75p ☐

Alan Williams

The Widow's War	95p ☐
Shah-Mak	95p ☐
Gentleman Traitor	60p ☐
The Béria Papers	75p ☐
Barbouze	£1.25 ☐
Long Run South	85p ☐
Snake Water	£1.25 ☐
The Purity League	85p ☐
The Tale of the Lazy Dog	85p ☐

THE WORLDS GREATEST NOVELISTS
NOW AVAILABLE IN GRANADA PAPERBACKS

John O'Hara

Ourselves to Know	£1.50	☐
Ten North Frederick	£1.50	☐
A Rage to Live	£1.50	☐
From The Terrace	£2.50	☐
BUtterfield 8	95p	☐
Appointment in Samarra	95p	☐

Norman Mailer

The Fight (non-fiction)	75p	☐
The Presidential Papers	95p	☐
Barbary Shore	40p	☐
Advertisements for Myself	95p	☐
An American Dream	£1.25	☐
The Naked and The Dead	£1.50	☐
The Deer Park	£1.75	☐

Kingsley Amis

Ending Up	60p	☐
The Riverside Villas Murder	95p	☐
I Like It Here	50p	☐
That Uncertain Feeling	50p	☐
Girl 20	40p	☐
I Want It Now	60p	☐
The Green Man	95p	☐
The Alteration	95p	☐

THE WORLD'S GREATEST THRILLER WRITERS – NOW AVAILABLE IN GRANADA PAPERBACKS

Trevanian

The Loo Sanction	£1.25 ☐
The Eiger Sanction	95p ☐
The Main	95p ☐

Gerald A. Browne

Slide	75p ☐
11 Harrowhouse	£1.25 ☐
Hazard	75p ☐

Robert Rosenblum

The Sweetheart Deal	85p ☐
The Good Thief	75p ☐

All these books are available at your local bookshop or newsagent, or can be ordered direct from the publisher. Just tick the titles you want and fill in the form below.

Name...

Address..

....

Write to Granada Cash Sales, PO Box 11, Falmouth, Cornwall TR10 9EN.

Please enclose remittance to the value of the cover price plus:

UK: 30p for the first book, 15p for the second book plus 12p per copy for each additional book ordered to a maximum charge of £1.29.

BFPO and EIRE: 30p for the first book, 15p for the second book plus 12p per copy for the next 7 books, thereafter 6p per book.

OVERSEAS: 50p for the first book and 15p for each additional book.

Granada Publishing reserve the right to show new retail prices on covers which may differ from those previously advertised in the text or elsewhere.